Praise for the novels of
LYNNE KAUFMAN

"Lynne Kaufman has the wisdom to understand that
the spiritual and sexual needs of women are really
inseparable, and the narrative skills to make
this forbidden truth a fascinating novel."
—_New York Times_ bestselling author
Tom Robbins on _Slow Hands_

"A totally one-of-a-kind mystery. The story of the
death and cover-up is sure to grab you."
—_Romance Reviews Today_ on _Wild Women's Weekend_

"Equal parts suspense and black comedy,
Wild Women's Weekend is slick and
seamlessly constructed."
—_Romantic Times_

"A smart, intricately woven story that dares to
challenge the norms of society. Filled with
courage and uncharacteristic approaches…
Slow Hands will make you stop and think."
—_The Word on Romance_

"Lynne Kaufman has brought psyche
and sensuality together in this absorbing
and imaginative women's novel."
—Jean Shinoda Bolen, M.D., author of
Goddesses in Everywoman

"A delightful story with many layers…
Highly entertaining with a provocative plot,
Slow Hands kept me amused with its effortless
writing. A perfect summer read."
—_Romance Reviews Today_

"Riotous…_Slow Hands_ is about every woman's
longing to be adored."
—_Woman's Own_ magazine

TAKING FLIGHT

LYNNE KAUFMAN

MIRA®

ISBN 0-7783-2188-6

TAKING FLIGHT

www.MIRABooks.com

Printed in U.S.A.

First Printing: December 2005
10 9 8 7 6 5 4 3 2 1

With abiding love to my family:
past, present and future.

1

Departures.

Julia awoke with a start, clawing her way out of a panic dream, with broken images hanging like cobwebs on her lashes. A drowning dream, gasping for breath; in one arm she held the children, babies again, valiantly keeping their sputtering mouths above water, in the other a trailing string bag from which objects floated: her passport, traveler's checks, itinerary, vouchers.

She huddled into a ball, digging deeper into the familiar comfort of her own sheets. Responding to her movement, Mark slid over to her side of the double bed, laced his arms around her, fitted his body spoon fashion against hers. She sighed and let her head rest on his shoulder. Encouraged, he moved his hands to cup her breasts. Deftly, she shifted her position, evading his grasp. It was reassurance she wanted, not lovemaking. "I had a terrible dream," she said. "I was losing everything. It must be anxiety about the trip."

He nuzzled her neck. "Then stay home. You know I'd prefer it."

"I have to go," she said. "It's part of my job. It's just that so many things can go wrong."

That was his cue to play comforter, appeaser of doubts. "Everything is organized. You know your lectures backward and forward. The travel agent will handle the logistics and you'll have two glorious weeks in the Aegean as a single lady."

"With thirty college sophomores," she amended.

"Thirty chaperones," he said.

"*I'm* the chaperone." This was the first trip she had taken without Mark. She thought back over the travels they had been on together in their twenty years of marriage, how Mark had always chosen the site, planned their stay, never for longer than the ten days he felt it safe to leave his medical practice. He had bought the guide books, the maps, chosen the hotels, choreographed the itinerary—always a balance of indoor and outdoor, physical and aesthetic activities. He'd studied the money, the customs, the language, doctored her queasy stomach and airplane sinusitis. Traveling with Mark had been like cruising in a chauffeur-driven limo, the windows discreetly open to passing sights and sounds.

But now she had pushed wide that heavily upholstered door and stepped outside onto the steaming pavement, amid the buses and trucks and jostling crowds. She had become a pedestrian. An independent traveler. Solo. Free. But free for what? The pleasures of Greece, she hoped. She had never been there, but had long studied its history, mythology and theater with great interest and enjoyment. Indeed, next year she would be teaching Greek tragedy, and the trip was a preparation for that.

She had never managed a tour group before, but Sabrina, the dean's secretary, was coming along to help. And then there would be Michael, her co-instructor, an actor and director, whom she hoped would provide good adult company. She could imagine them discussing the role of the Greek chorus over a glass of retsina in a picturesque seaside tavern.

And there was something more. An ever growing, disturbing question about her life, her marriage. She would have two weeks to think about it without the demands of everyday life. She would be visiting the site of the Oracle of Delphi, where the ancient Greeks had asked for guidance for their most difficult dilemmas. She would do the same and hope for an answer. Perhaps in that sacred place she could contact the source of a deeper wisdom.

Julia's reverie was interrupted by a familiar weight of sixty pounds landing on her hip. She stirred to find Wendy, her mirror image at age nine, chocolate-brown eyes riveted to hers.

"Are you leaving today?" her daughter demanded. Julia nodded. Wendy flung her weight like a sinker, burrowing into her mother's belly. "I don't want you to." A wiry, long-limbed, puckish child, she had amber freckled skin, a jutting aquiline nose, Indian-straight hair. "Well, you certainly can't deny that one," people would say when they saw them together. Who would want to? Not now. Once, Julia thought, once long ago, during that dark time. Now she delighted in the resemblance and spent long times of pleasure absorbed in the little girl's expressive face and movements.

It was hard won, that acceptance of self: a year of psychotherapy, of weekly meetings with Dr. Liston, a year of sobbing into his brown Naugahyde chair, of mood elevating drugs, confessions of misdeeds, of wrong thoughts, shameful desires, and long recitals of her inadequacies…her tiny breasts, her troubled skin, her lack of courage, discipline, generosity, love. Finally, she had come through the tunnel of depression, of swirling sawtoothed thoughts, even one stagy suicide attempt with a handful of sleeping pills, to arrive at a form of equilibrium. She had begun therapy in tears of despair and ended it with an appreciative handshake. Eight years since that parting, longer since the catastrophic depression, but she still wondered about its unopened message. Was that dark time simply a result of postpartum hormones or did it augur more? And why was she thinking about it now?

Julia threw off the covers and climbed out of bed. As she opened the curtains, the Los Angeles sunshine flooded the room. After a long, hot shower she entered the kitchen. As she cracked an egg against the rim of a bowl, she noticed her hands trembling. She made no attempt to still them; all risk, all growth came with such stirrings. She remembered a quote from the poet Roethke: "This shaking keeps me steady, I should know. I learn by going where I have to go." The advantage of a literary education, she thought wryly, an existential quote for any occasion. Even though they were usually sad.

She measured milk and oil into the pancake batter for a hot, hearty, well-balanced breakfast. She slid bacon slices into a frying pan, wincing as the fat splattered, leaving a garland of grease upon the stove. She cut juicy oranges into quarters. Other mothers did this daily, she reflected, sending their families out with filled bellies and home-cooked love, while she made do with packaged muffins and sugar-coated cereals. Other mothers, other wives...old rusty nails in the sepulcher of unworthiness. She thrust those thoughts from her.

As a bonus of psychotherapy, she had relinquished the dream of perfect motherhood. Over Mark's strong and repeated objections, she had gone back to school for a master's degree, obtained it, and shortly after found a teaching position at a nearby woman's college.

Now dust gathered under the beds, hair clogged the drains, clothes tangled in closets, fingerprints embroidered doors. Frozen vegetables, bottled dressings, bakery cookies were served. The children were put in charge of their own baths, homework and social schedules. She had moved from teaching two classes a week to a full-time appointment, and with teaching, student conferences, faculty committees and lecture preparation, she was gone from nine till four like a grown-up, and was paid for it in money, status and stress.

The family set the table in a smooth and wordless ritual. Mark laid place mats and crockery; Wendy added silverware and carefully folded paper napkins. Davey, with adolescent aplomb, balanced the milk, orange juice, maple syrup and newspaper. They each sat in their accustomed seat. Mark divided the newspaper—sports and business for himself, entertainment section for Davey. Julia received the main section; Wendy still needed to look at what she was eating.

"Quite a spread," Mark commented.

"The plane doesn't leave until eleven," she explained. "I had time to cook."

"Well, you're off duty for two weeks now," he added as he folded a bacon strip and pushed it into his already full mouth.

Julia watched his pumping jaws and felt a wave of distaste. Had he always eaten that way or had she just begun to notice? It was the same way he made love—noisy, rushed, aggressive. She tried to push the thoughts from her. She did not want to feel critical today, only kind, accepting. When had this shadow side come into prominence? Sometimes he looked good to her, craggy and virile. But at other times all she saw were his sagging jowls, uneven teeth, the dark circles beneath the pale blue eyes. Had he become plain, uncomely, or was she simply projecting the dissatisfaction she felt? Was it the unresolved conflicts, the buried resentments that scarred him for her? He had never really accepted her working, having her own life. Furthermore he had objected to her seeing women friends or pursuing hobbies in her free time, anything that took her further away from him and the family. They had reached a sort of truce about it. At least they had stopped fighting. But there was a residual chill between them. They were careful with each other. Moments of spontaneity, of intimacy, were rare.

Ironically, in stormy seas with danger or crisis throughout, she rarely questioned the ship of their marriage, just
held on to its railings for survival, grateful for its shelter,
its solidity. But when the angry waves subsided and the
sun shone, she looked about its confines, its cracking
paint, frayed ropes and mildewed cabin, and the stretch
of open sea invited—cool, sparkling, bearing palm
fringed islands ripe for exploring. More and more, lately,
she had felt restless and unhappy.

A memory of the first time she had seen Mark came
flooding back. That first imprinting. A blind date, arranged by a cousin. "He's a medical resident," she had
been told, "Jewish and tall."

"But what does he look like?" she had asked.

"He's tall and he's a doctor," the girl had repeated.
"What more do you want?"

Both her mother and her best girlfriend had echoed
the same sentiment. "You're so lucky. What a catch!" And
she had thought so, too, for a time.

Julia looked down at her breakfast plate. It was empty.
Unknowingly, she had cut, chewed, swallowed. She
began clearing plates, stacking them.

She busied herself in going over the arrangements
one more time with Mark. "You can make hamburgers
twice a week. Then one night each of pork chops,
chicken breasts and steak. Just broil them," she said.

"Noodles, spaghetti, rice and potatoes are in the cabinet. Lots of frozen vegetables—the kids won't eat them but serve them anyway. Ice cream and fruit for dessert. One night you can do soup and sandwiches, one night eat out. The cleaning woman comes every Tuesday, I've paid her in advance. Wendy will ride the bus home from day camp with Davey. They'll get home about five. If Wendy is sick, there's a list of four sitters. Mrs. Glick is expensive but she's the most reliable. Water the plants once a week. My itinerary and contact information is by the phone, also Barbara's number and Janine's if you get stuck. They both said they'd invite you to dinner one night."

"I don't need their charity, thank you," Mark said.

"It's not charity. They just want to help."

"They're your friends, not mine," he stated.

"Well, why don't you call your friends, then?"

"They're guys I play tennis with and guys I practice medicine with. We don't have dinner together." Mark glanced at the kitchen clock. "Twenty after eight."

Davey pushed the last pancake into his mouth, gulped his milk. "Get a move on, Wen."

Obediently, the little girl jumped up, grabbed her sweatshirt. "Where's our lunch?" she asked.

"Oh, God, I forgot to make them," Julia said. "It'll only take a second."

"There's no time, Mom." Davey flung on his backpack. "We'll miss the bus."

"You have to eat lunch," she argued.

"We'll bum some off the other kids," he said. "No problem."

Julia pulled at her son's sleeve as he darted for the door. "Take care of yourself and don't forget to write. Dad has my address."

As she leaned forward, the boy averted his head slightly so that her kiss grazed his cheek. "Gotta run," he cried.

She circled Wendy around the waist, brushed the hair off her daughter's face and planted a kiss on each cheek. "I love you, dumpling," she said.

The little girl returned the hug, then squirmed from her embrace. "I gotta go, Mom. Hey, Davey, wait up."

"So much for tearful farewells," she said, glancing ruefully at Mark. Her plan had been for a peaceful, nurturing morning, an affectionate goodbye with unhurried private dialogue. Instead the children were off with their teeth and hair unbrushed. Unmothered, unlunched…

She turned back toward the sink and began soaping the dishes. In clearing the table, Mark had jammed one glass inside another so tightly that it smashed as she separated them. A bad omen. Mark remained at the table, riffling through the newspaper. The house was strangely silent. Usually when the children left, she would quickly tidy up and finish dressing, he would call his answering service for messages, and they would both leave for work. Mornings when Mark did not have a conference or she an early class were awkward, for the possibility of going back to bed loomed large, especially if she had refused or evaded sex for a week or more. Then the unspoken demand rumbled like an underground quake. Lately she had been dressing before breakfast to forestall it, even though the best time for lovemaking was early in the morning while she was still veiled in the last vestiges of sleep, warm and drifting in dreams, before the knife of memory and judgment interceded.

She scoured the dishes as if purifying them, scrubbed with fury at old baked spots on pot bottoms. Swabbed the table, swept the floor meticulously. While Mark shaved, she changed all the bed linen, paired shoes and laid them neatly in the bottom of closets. She dressed for traveling in a newly purchased sky-blue linen pantsuit, more stylish than practical. Its fabric would crease and show stains, but it was new and youthful and would reveal her still-slender waist and long legs.

She dabbed a light lavender scent on her wrists and throat. It had been a birthday present from her mother. She would be spending the next few nights in her parents' New York apartment, where her mother was recovering from her latest surgery. The procedure had revealed that the cancer had spread. Once again Julia would be immersed in the sorrow and pain of her mother's illness, helpless to affect its outcome.

Eyes downcast, as if curtaining her thoughts, she entered the living room. Mark dropped the newspaper to the rug, inviting but not initiating talk. Instead, she moved across the room, attending to the crushed sofa cushions, the sprinkling of crumbs on the coffee table, the scattered playing cards. She busied herself repairing the disarray, setting the room to rights. External order containing the turmoil within. The silence pulsated between them, the unasked questions…insistent as static jamming the bland Muzak they usually spoke.

"All set?" Mark asked finally. "Did you weigh your bags?"

"I'm only taking the big brown one. I won't need much. It's summer."

"About the same climate as New York." He consulted the paper. "Eighty-seven in New York yesterday. Ninety-four in Athens."

"Hot," she said.

"And you don't respond well to heat. Did you pack salt pills?"

"I forgot," she said. "Do we have any?"

"Let me check my medical bag," he said, eager to

move, to be useful. "You've got to take better care of yourself."

Julia sat and stared at the newly vacated chair, his chair, the red chair, and remembered a similar admonition eight years ago, the day after Wendy was born.

It was a private room at Children's Hospital; she was propped up on two starched white pillows, still light-headed and dry-mouthed from the Demerol, her bottom stiff and burning from the episiotomy, breasts throbbing, brain racing with fears and visions. A girl, a daughter. Julia had somehow been certain that this baby would be a boy like her first, whom she would tend but would later turn over to Mark for identity, for values. But this baby was a girl, and she would have to be the role model. She was not womanly enough for a daughter. Fantasy demands of perfection roared in her head, of having to teach this infant girl to cook and clean with dispatch, to walk and dress with grace, to style her hair, to skillfully apply makeup…although she herself had not been so taught, nor fully learned. She felt unable, unwilling, inadequate.

Oh, God, not to be thrust back into the house again, to have the front door slam shut like a vault. To have the days structured by feedings and diaper changes and the constant siren of a baby's wails. She couldn't bear to be housebound again, roped to the yoke of mothering…the victim of a five-year robbery, her freedom, her independence stolen. And even if she could somehow find the money and energy to secure a stand-in, there was no substituting for herself, no appeasement for the constant guilt of absence.

And why was there no joy in sharing this child with Mark? There had been the first time, with Davey, seven years ago. Why was there now no love for this man, no sense of union, of family, of fulfillment? Why was there no satisfaction when the doctor beamed and said the baby looked just like her? Please, someone take this child away, a voice in her head had screamed. I can't do this.

And yet when the tiny creature, swaddled in pink, was laid in her arms, the contact released a torrent of tears, of love and tenderness for the baby, for the world, for Mark and for herself. She'd longed to talk to him honestly, intimately. Longed to break through the wall that divided them, to recapture the closeness they'd once had.

He had brought her flowers, a dozen white carnations, scentless and hardy, instead of the few red roses or yellow tulips she would have preferred, and thrust them in her hand, avoiding her eyes. She had tried to talk to him, to tell him how sad and frightened she felt. How unequal to the task before her. But instead of hearing her out, he had blurted, "You've got to take better care of yourself," and immediately launched into the details of his just completed tennis tournament.

It was a Sunday; still smelling of acrid dried sweat, he had come in tennis clothes, a pair of wrinkled khakis pulled on over his shorts. He'd reported on the match, which had gone three sets. He and his partner had won the third in a sudden-death tiebreaker. He'd been flushed with victory, and quickly launched into a talking reverie, reliving the major points, the great "gets," the crucial double faults, the dubious line calls, of how pleased he was with his courage to poach on the final shot rather than playing it safe.

He had reached into his zippered bag, proudly removed a small silver-plated cup and placed it on the coverlet. "Of course, it has to be engraved," he'd said.

"Of course," she agreed, "and we can put it with the others."

He had smiled contentedly then and asked, "So what do you want to name the baby?"

Her reverie faded as Mark returned to the living room with a vial of salt pills. She tucked them into her purse, amid the stomach remedies, the aspirin, the antihistamines. Mark carried her suitcase to the car and they were silent on the short ride to the airport, listening to the radio news. It was in the shadowy airport garage that she decided to tell him about Michael, quickly, awkwardly, like a foot shoved in a door.

"Did I mention that Michael Carpenter is going?"

"Going where?" Mark asked.

"To Greece, as a guest lecturer. You know how he teaches for us sometimes when he's in between a film or a play. Well, he's just finished shooting—we're really lucky to get him. The girls are thrilled. They're all madly in love with him."

"What does he know about Greece?"

"It's not Greece so much, it's a theater tour. He'll be talking about acting and directing. Adding a touch of glamour."

She went on, helpless to stop, embroidering, embellishing. "He'll provide a good balance, actually."

Actually... Even her word choice was stilted, contrived. "I'll do the history and literature part and he can critique the interpretation and production. Give the girls a well-rounded picture. He can share the responsibility, too. It'll be useful having another grown-up along."

"What about your assistant?" Mark hoisted the heavy suitcase onto the moving sidewalk.

"Sabrina? She's only a kid herself. She won't be much help."

"Then why bring her along?" he pressed.

"She can do some of the routine stuff, distributing

room keys, counting heads on the bus, things like that," Julia said. She is coming along to free me to be with a grown-up some of the time. An intelligent, attractive man who has similar interests. Someone to talk to, maybe even to flirt with. Someone with whom I can feel like a woman again.

Mark surrendered the suitcase at the weigh-in desk. There was a flurry of document exchange and keyboard entries, and then they moved aside for a farewell.

"Give your parents my best," Mark said. "Your mom should be up and around by the time you get there."

"I will," Julia said. Then, in a whisper, she added, "I'm so worried about her. Tell me the truth. I know it's bad…but she's not going to die, is she?" The question could have been posed weeks ago, anytime following Mark's phone consultations with her mother's surgeon and oncologist, but Julia had saved it for the anonymity and urgency of the airport, the concealing bustle of hundreds of comings and goings.

"Your mother's had a radical mastectomy," Mark said, his voice level, his tone thoughtful. "There was contagion and it spread to the lymph glands. Tissue and muscle were removed, now only time will tell."

Julia listened as if mesmerized; Mark's whole persona had changed. His face was strong and composed, selfless, heroic…the mask of the physician. It was what had drawn her to him as a girl of twenty, that promise of wisdom, judgment, protection, his connection with an ancient, respected tradition, a repository of all the healing knowledge of the tribe. The shaman, the medicine man. Marry him and step inside his circle of power. She had loved Mark's hands—his long, slender fingers, his pale scrubbed nails. How they could wield a scalpel, suture a wound, probe and palpate, unearth the source of pain and disease. She'd loved the sure way he laid his hand upon the pulse beat, the distended belly, the fiery boil, the running sore. The hands of a healer. She had studied them in the half-light of candles as they caressed her body, and she'd been thrilled by his touch as if by a forbidden rite.

Impulsively, she now took one of his large cool hands in both of hers and drew it to her lips. When she released it she saw his eyes were moist with tears. Moved, she leaned forward for his kiss, permitting her lips to soften, to part. Misconstruing, he pressed hard, thrusting his tongue into her mouth. She pulled back, startled. She wanted tenderness, communion, not a sexual overture. They stared across the space, a sad familiar chasm. She bridged the gap with a quick conciliatory peck, a wave, and strode off briskly toward the boarding gate.

Julia took her assigned window seat on the plane and opened the collected works of Sophocles. Reaching the recognition scene in *Oedipus Rex* and the limits of her concentration simultaneously, she spent the next few hours channel surfing the audio and video offerings and gazing out the window. When the dinner tray was proffered, she ate only the dessert. Drinking the complimentary tepid chardonnay, she thought about the upcoming trip, about her mother, about Mark. Everything seemed to be in flux. Even her job, a former constant, no longer satisfied her the way it used to.

For her last classroom session, she had chosen Chekhov's play *Three Sisters*, wanting its theme of the clash of old and new values to end the year with its bittersweet melody. But her class had shared none of her empathy for the ravages of fate, the inequities of time. Her students had felt no pathos in the sisters' plight of being well-educated women trapped in a dreary Russian village, only impatience at their self-pity, their inability to act. "If they think Moscow is so great," one girl had flatly announced, "let them get on the train."

In this age of bottom line, the message was clear, Julia thought. Take responsibility for your own life.

2

As Julia alighted from the plane at Kennedy Airport, she saw her father in the front row of the waiting throng and felt the familiar lift of connection in her throat and chest. He looked pale, grayer, more troubled; he must have been there for hours harkening back to the days when air travel was of great moment. As she walked down the runway she met his eyes obliquely; it was too soon to confront directly the gaze of those chocolate-brown eyes that mirrored her own. Her eyes were her beauty spot, men had said, liquid, mutable, flecked with gold, fringed by straight black lashes. Her father's eyes. Her father's nose, too, she thought ruefully, too long and broad for her oval face. Her father's skin, volatile, subject to eruption and, like a battle map, retaining all the markings of past strife.

Handbag swinging off her shoulder, she hugged him

clumsily, a partial, decorous embrace, only their arms and shoulders touching. She had a sudden memory of being held, cradled in her father's lap, a gangly girl of six or seven. Every Sunday morning he would read the funny pages to her…Blondie, Little Orphan Annie, Nancy and Sluggo. That particular Sunday she had slept late, recovering from a winter cold; he had been by her bedside, dissolving a sulfur packet in a tablespoon of applesauce, when they'd heard a loud rumble, the sound of an avalanche or an earthquake. They had run into the living room and found their red chair was buried beneath a mountain of smoking plaster, of shattered wooden beams. The ceiling had caved in, instantly, without warning. Had they been sitting there, they would have been injured or worse. When they had finally fixed the ceiling, replaced the red chair, it was decided that she was old enough to read the comics herself.

Julia felt her father's appraising glance. "You look good, darling," he said. "How are things at home? Mark? The children?"

"They're fine, Dad, everything's fine. Mark's practice is going well. He's heading up lots of hospital committees. Davey's made the tennis team and he's discovered girls. Wendy's learning piano."

Her father nodded. "Sounds like everyone's keeping busy."

To him, it mattered less what she said than how she said it, for he could hear the melody beneath her words, the pattern of her breath, the holding and the release. Like the time he had called her a few days after Wendy was born, a routine paternal call. How was she? How was the baby? She had summoned her best energy, cheer, anecdotes, the same protective cover she showed to the world. He had listened, but then had quietly asked, "Julia, are you all right?" The strength of his concern was like his hand laid upon her cheek, and she had been helpless to stop the tears.

"I'm just tired," she had sobbed. "Not getting enough sleep."

"Get someone to help with the baby," he had urged.

"It'll be okay."

"I'll send you the money," he said firmly.

"No, really, don't." The thought had brought a wry smile; she and Mark had much more money than her parents had ever had.

"I'll call you tomorrow," her father had said.

And he had called every day at noon, for a month, until the rhythm of her voice assured him that she was on the mend. That was the same month she had begun therapy.

Her father retrieved her brown leather suitcase from the revolving rack and, reeling a bit from its weight, joked, "What did you bring, the Golden Gate Bridge?"

Nevertheless, he insisted upon carrying it through the air-conditioned terminal and out into the steamy heat of the July evening. Familiar New York summer weather, Julia thought. The asphalt on the roadway oozed, the air was thick with exhaust, men wiped their foreheads with already damp handkerchiefs.

She waited until they were seated in the car, windows opened to a faint, sooty breeze, before asking, "How's Mom doing?"

"She's feeling a little better today," he replied. "That last transfusion helped. With the painkillers and sedatives, she's able to sleep, and when she's up to it, we sit on the terrace or go for a drive." He summoned a smile. "The best sign is she's talking on the phone again."

"What do the doctors say?"

He concentrated upon his driving, easing the car into the passing lane, then back again with carefully calibrated turns of the wheel. He had learned to drive at fifty, Julia remembered, when the factory where he had been foreman for twenty years closed, and he had taken a job on the road, driving country highways in Massachusetts and Connecticut selling women's clothing from a mail-order catalog. He had given that up, though, when her mother got ill.

He lighted a cigarette and inhaled deeply. "What do the doctors know? Sometimes I feel sorry for them. So many questions. So few answers. The cancer is spreading. That much we all know. They had hoped to get it all out with the mastectomy, but they didn't. So first it was radiation, then chemo. But every drug has complications, side effects…anemia, edema."

The words washed over Julia like an Indian chant, a raga. The message was clear but the language alien. Her father, whose previous medical knowledge had consisted of identifying the flu and the grippe, now had become doctor and nurse.

They spent the rest of the time in companionable silence, driving through the streets of the East Bronx as twilight tinged the sky and softened the air. Julia gazed at the landings and steps of the tenements teeming with people; bare brown arms and legs swaying to the blare of transistorized rock; babies nursing; children improvising street games with manhole covers and broomstick bats; lovers kissing and stroking; drunken men crumpled on the sidewalk with glazed eyes and urine stained pants. The streets were piled with garbage, strewn with dog turds and broken glass. The air was filled with the aroma of chili peppers and the lilt of barrio puertoriqueño.

Her father turned the car onto the Grand Concourse, once a seat of great elegance. Immigrants from the ghettos of the Lower East Side, who had risen in the ranks of night school to become accountants and furriers and periodontists, had brought their two-child families to four-room apartments overlooking the Concourse. It was the Champs-Élysées of the Bronx, with its broad tree-lined avenues, redbrick synagogues and kosher-style restaurants with white linen tablecloths. Now, though, the once proud Concourse Towers with its uniformed doorman had become a welfare hotel for transients and even the corner Safeway had closed, a victim of pilferage and vandalism.

Her father parked the car and they entered the apartment house elevator. He nodded to the two other occupants but exchanged no words. "We should move," her mother had said the last time Julia had visited. "We don't know anyone here anymore. But how can we afford it? Where could we go?"

The hall to the apartment was stifling and smelled of fish. At the apartment door, her father dropped the suitcase to fit his key into the lock. "Don't be surprised when you see her," he warned.

Her mother was lying on the sofa. As they entered, she struggled to sit up. Julia suppressed a gasp. It had only been six months since her last visit. It was her hair, she realized, the chemo. Then her mother had had carefully coiffed strawberry-blond waves. Now, only a few wisps of white froth remained.

Her mother's hand darted to her brow. "I have a wig,"

she said, her voice dry and hoarse. "But it's so heavy it hurts my head. I only wear it when we go out."

"It's fine. Mom, you look fine," Julia protested.

"You're not used to seeing me this way." Her mother shrugged. "I'm not used to seeing myself this way."

"I'm just glad to see you, that's all."

"You must be hungry. Sid," she called, "make her something to eat."

Her father returned from putting away the suitcase. "You want to hang up some of your clothes?"

"No rush, Dad. I'll do it later."

"You hungry?" he continued. "Want something to eat?"

"No, thanks. I ate on the plane."

"Make some coffee, Sid. Put out the marble cake." Julia's mother smiled at her. "You see, I remembered you like marble cake."

Do I? Julia wondered. Once I must have. "Great," she said. "I haven't had Gideon's marble cake in years."

"What about you, Bea?" Sid turned to his wife. "What are you going to have?"

"Me? What can I have? Nothing has any taste."

"Then it doesn't matter," he said firmly. He poured a glass of orange juice, added a straw and brought it to her. "Drink," he said, "you need lots of fluids."

"I'm so bloated," her mother complained, but she sighed and sucked on the straw.

Julia watched as her father opened the kitchen cabinet and removed the small metal percolator. "Is anyone going to have seconds on coffee?" he asked.

"Who knows yet? Put up the big one," her mother called. "So help me," she whispered to Julia, "since he retired, he's driving me crazy."

Soon the aroma of percolating coffee wafted on the air. "Don't forget the saucers," her mother called.

"We don't have to be so fancy," he answered. "It's only family."

"Why can't you use saucers when I ask?" her mother protested.

"Bea, when you set the table, you use saucers. When I set the table I don't."

Julia watched as he laid saucers beneath two cups, his own stubbornly bare. The familiarity of her parents' banter was comforting. They still had the energy for the minor skirmishes. Not everything had changed. Julia glanced about the familiar apartment, the same furnishings she had grown up with—the overstuffed furniture, the end tables laden with family photographs, the porcelain lamps with their yellowing shades still protected by plastic dustcovers.

"Coffee's ready, Bea," Sid said, pouring his wife a steaming cup. "Get a move on."

Julia waited while her mother laboriously moved from

a lying to a sitting position, then, gripping the arm of the sofa, slowly stood, uncertain, weaving.

"Mom," she said, reaching out to her, "can I help you?"

"I'm all right. I just get a little dizzy when I get up too fast." Bea drew her robe tightly around her and with a slow, tremulous gait walked the few steps to the table. She took the nearest chair and sank down heavily.

Bea watched with approval as Julia drank two cups of strong coffee, each accompanied by a slice of thickly frosted marble cake. At her mother's insistence, her father brought out a heavily laden fruit bowl, and they lingered at the table, slicing peaches and honeydew melon. First they talked about Julia's family, then the extended family, some family friends, the long transmigrated neighbors, the neighbors' children, their marriages and divorces, all to the background drone of the TV. Finally, after the sign-off of the eleven o'clock news, with its ritual reports of carnage and crime, her father yawned, scratched his ample belly and stated, "Good night, girls, I'm leaving you." He leaned over and pressed a kiss to his wife's forehead.

Bea placed her palm tenderly against his cheek. Then she added, "Don't forget to shave tomorrow."

"Yeah, yeah," he said as he headed for the bedroom. Julia recalled the old Borscht Belt joke, when does a double positive equal a negative.

The news segued into Jay Leno, and against the background of his opening monologue, the Hollywood guests, the insistent commercials, Julia and her mother talked, or rather Julia listened as her mother spoke. The theme was injustice, often her mother's theme—the unfairness of life. Ever since she was a little girl Julia remembered hearing about why Bea, the smartest, sweetest, most honorable of the four sisters, was the least rewarded; why Bea had had to go to secretarial school to support the family and not go to college; why Sid had never made the money that other husbands had; why their apartment didn't look out to the street; why Bea, the good one who never argued, never complained, always got the short straw.

But the anger that had flared in Julia as a child and adolescent, listening to those woes, that fiery charge to do something about it, was banked now. Tonight she listened with a calm sadness to a tale of universal longing and loss. We all have regrets. She, too, had amassed a store of poor decisions, bad luck, actions not taken.

Her mother's talk shifted to more current ills—to her part-time job of ten years; to her boss, that bastard, who hadn't even given her severance pay; and to her lifetime friend who wouldn't visit because illness depressed her. And the doctor, that rotten internist. Here her mother's voice rose in outrage. "That man neglected me. I complained about pain in my right breast for two years. He kept telling me it was nothing. He should have taken X-rays. Two years. You remember when we came out to California for Davey's bar mitzvah? I told you I was having pain."

Julia nodded. The information must have somehow gotten lost in the tangle of half-remembered conversations.

"No," her mother corrected, "I never told you. I didn't want to upset you. Finally they took an X-ray. They cut off my breast, but it was too late. Much too late." Bea opened her robe and Julia forced herself to not turn away. On one side of her mother's chest there was a soft heavy breast, on the other a desert of burned, puckered skin bordered with red scars marking the incision.

Her mother fingered the wound. "It's healing. I've been doing the exercises the therapist taught me. Reach for the ceiling." She demonstrated, slowly raising her arm above her head, then lowering it. "Well," she said with a wince, "with my arthritis, it wasn't so good before the operation." She closed her robe. "Losing my breast wasn't so terrible. After all, like Dad says, I'm no spring chicken. But now—" her voice lowered "—who knows?"

"But Mom, it's in remission. They're discovering new drugs every day. You look fine, you're getting stronger."

Tears veiled Bea's eyes as she reached for her daughter's hand. "Live, Julia," she said. "I never did."

Julia gripped her mother's hand, massaging the cold slender fingers. Live, she thought. Yes, of course. But how?

The remaining days of her visit were spent in synchrony with her mother's timetable. Frequent small meals, daytime talk shows, an afternoon nap, an occasional outing to a nearby park bench. And lots of meandering talk, cloudy reminiscences, her mother's mild inquiries about Mark, the children, her job. Although Julia's thoughts often drifted back to the troubled state of her marriage, she kept those worries to herself. She was here to provide comfort. Mostly they just sat together, she and her mother, and it was enough. Julia told her mom a story she had heard about a four-year-old who visited a neighbor who had lost his wife. The little boy had immediately climbed upon the man's lap.

"What did you say to Mr. Schwartz?" the boy's mother had later asked.

"Nothing," the boy said. "I just helped him cry."

"That's a good story," Bea had said. She took Julia's hand and kissed it.

At six on the morning of her departure, her father's knock sounded on the door. "I'm up," Julia called. Indeed, she had been awake since four, after dozing fitfully all night, assailed by memories and fragments of illusive dreams. She had awoken with a sympathetic pain in her right breast, missing Mark's familiar presence and rhythmic breathing, yet with growing excitement as she thought of the coming trip.

She dressed hurriedly in the same outfit she had arrived in, blue linen pantsuit and strappy sandals, then glanced around the bedroom. It was just as she had left it twenty years ago. Her high school and college diplomas hung beside the mirror; her textbooks lined the bookshelves: Shakespeare, Dickinson and Frost; Sartre and Camus, Plato and Kierkegaard resting next to the novels of Roth and Bellow, Malamud and Singer.

She opened the top drawer of her dresser and rummaged through her grammar school autograph book, turning to a stenciled heart that read, "First comes love, then comes marriage, then comes Julia with a baby carriage." But what happens when you fall out of love? she thought. Is that what she was experiencing now? Would she ever feel desire again? Ever feel desirable again?

Under the autograph book lay a white angora sweater she had once kept in the refrigerator, like whipped cream, to preserve its fluffiness. Next to the sweater was a yellowing horsehair crinoline and her wedding veil, a corona of white plastic lilies of the valley trailing yards of white tulle.

In the bottom drawer was a garter belt, stockings with embroidered clocks on the ankle, a charm bracelet, a rolled up pair of white bobby sox, an eyelash curler, a dried up tube of Clearasil and a plastic box of rubber tipped bobby pins for her nightly pincurls. A time capsule of her life before marriage. She stood before the mirror in the growing light and brushed her dark hair back from her face. Strange how, when she had finally decided to stop curling her hair, it had developed its own natural wave, irregular but soft and flattering. "A woman's hair should frame her face like the petals of a flower," Colette, the great romance novelist, had once said. And who would know better, Julia thought.

When she came out of the bathroom, her father was waiting. "I just made coffee," he said. "We can get something to eat at the airport."

"Fine," she said, sipping from the cup he offered her. "It's too early to chew."

"You never were hungry in the morning." He watched her finish the cup. "Ready to go?"

She nodded. "Is Mom up? I'll say goodbye."

"She had a bad night. I gave her a sedative. She's still asleep."

"I'll just get my purse, then." But as Julia tiptoed past the half-closed bedroom door, she heard her mother's faint call. She entered the room; although it was oppressively hot, Bea lay covered by a heavy quilt. Julia bent and kissed her cheek, breathing in the sweet-sour smell of fever. She embraced her carefully. The steroids had made her mother's bones fragile, her skin sensitive. "Take care, Mom," she whispered. "I'll be in touch. I've left my itinerary with Dad if you need me."

"Did you have breakfast?" her mother asked, her speech sleepy and slurred.

"I'll eat at the airport," Julia said.

"You could have eaten here," her mother protested. "Dad bought fresh bagels."

"I'll take one to Greece."

"It wouldn't be such a bad idea. The food they serve on those airplanes is for the birds."

Julia smiled; her mother had flown exactly twice, once to California for Davey's bar mitzvah and once back. "I'll put one in my pocket," she said, and closed the bedroom door behind her. I wish I could put you both in my pocket, she thought, as she and her father walked to the car. He looked so pale. He needed sun and clean air, brisk walks on a sandy beach, blue sky. He needed to be out of the caged apartment, out of the stagnant streets, the buffeting noise, the traffic. He needed to escape New York. Just as she had.

Mark had provided that escape. She had been ripe for the picking and he had chosen her. Early on, he had made it clear. Her combination of coltish good looks and quick mind had won him over, and she'd been young enough to be malleable. And for her, Mark was the genie's lamp, the magic wand transforming straw into gold. She would have a doctor husband, status and security; he would take care of her. For dowry, her hymen was gift enough. Did she love him? How could she have known? She was nineteen. A virgin, still living at home. She had had crushes on boys. But love? What was love?

"You don't have to marry him," her father had said as he noticed her tears on her wedding morning. But she did. They both knew she did. Just as now, as Sid appraised her thoughtful face and said, "You don't have to go, you know." But she did. She had made a commitment.

In the car, they talked about her cousin's divorce. "I don't understand young people today," her father said, lighting a cigarette. "They don't work at things. It's like the world owes them a living. If they don't get a raise, they quit their job. If their wife doesn't smell good in the morning, they get a divorce. In my time, marriage was for life. For better or worse, in sickness or in health. Divorce was for the rich. Poor people stayed married. They worked, they had kids, they made the best of it."

"Maybe you were lucky, Dad."

"I don't know about lucky. We never thought about it."

Julia was silent, staring at the heat fumes rising from the passing streets.

"You think it's always been so easy for your mother and me. It hasn't," he continued. "When we were starting out, we had to move in with your grandparents, seven people in three rooms. I finally got a job, but the factory closed soon after. I was out of work for a year. There were operations, sicknesses, but we managed." He glanced away. "You think my life is a picnic now?"

"You shouldn't stay home all the time, Dad. Mom's well enough to be left alone sometimes. You ought to get out, play some cards, go to a movie, take a walk."

He shook his head. "She gets frightened if I leave her. She can't breathe. I don't want to feel that I've neglected her in any way. It's better to be there."

He ground out his cigarette in the overflowing ashtray. "What is this love they all talk about?" he mused almost to himself. "When they say, 'I'm leaving because I don't love her anymore.' Do they mean sex? Is that what they mean?"

"I don't know, Dad."

"I think that's what they mean…sex." He glanced over at her appraisingly as if waiting for a response. She wondered if this conversation was prompted by some intuitive flash. Did her father once more sense that all was not right in her life? But this time she could not share her secret. He had troubles of his own. He drove onto the airport departure ramp.

Julia checked her watch. True to form, it was seven; the plane left at ten.

"Do you want me to wait with you?" he asked, hoisting her suitcase from the trunk.

"No, Dad, I'll be fine. You go ahead." She signaled to a waiting porter.

"What about breakfast?"

"I'm not hungry," she lied.

"You're sure?" He waited for her nod. "Then I'll go. Your mother will be getting up soon." He turned to face her. "It was good to see you, darling. Stay well."

"You, too, Dad." She embraced him closely; this time there was no distance, no barrier.

"Have a safe trip," he said. Then, thoughtfully, he asked, "Mark doesn't mind your being away?"

"He minds," she said, "a little."

"Good," he said, "he should."

Julia waved as her father drove off. Would Mark miss her? In practical matters, certainly. As for the rest, the separation might be a relief for him, as well. Too many nights of lying beside her barricaded body, her detached, floating consciousness. The times that she and Mark did make love she would eschew his probing kisses and focus instead on the impersonality of his body, for it was better than abstinence and helped to defuse the mounting tension, the glacier of rejection that would freeze them both in their beds.

These two weeks would help her to sort out her thoughts. Help her to make a decision. "Live, Julia," her mother had said. But how?

3

Julia checked her bag, then bought a copy of the *New York Times* and headed for the coffee shop. A sign informed her that booths were reserved for two persons or more. The world conspired against the single. Somehow she had always known that. Perhaps that was why she had married so young. She took a seat at the counter, which afforded inadequate space to read and eat in comfort, sipped her weak coffee and nibbled at the doughy muffin spread with meager squares of butter and grape jelly. Why, she wondered, was it always grape jelly, her least favorite?

Even after reading the *Times* from front to back, she still had a full hour until boarding time. Settling herself in the waiting area, she checked her purse. She opened her passport and admired its virtually unmarked pages. Only one sheet had been used, commemorating last year's anniversary trip to London, Paris and Rome. Mark had carefully planned the ten-day trip and they had stayed well, seen all the obligatory sites and had the photos and souvenirs to prove it. And yet for Julia that trip had been a blur, a confused rush of museums and monuments and restaurants. She had vowed this trip to Greece would be different, and she had planned the itinerary accordingly.

She opened the travel schedule she had prepared. Each day centered on one important site or activity. There would be a guided tour and then ample time to explore on one's own, to reflect, to imagine, to dream. Time to put the experience into a personal context, to generate feelings and lasting memories. The trip began in Athens, the capital and thriving hub of Greek society. She would have that evening to rest and recoup before the group arrived the next day, shepherded by Sabrina and Michael, and the program would begin in earnest.

A week in Athens and environs, then a week bus tour of the Peloponnese with stops at Mycenae and its fabled beehive tombs; Epidaurus and its ancient theater; Olympus, the site of the original Olympic Games and finally Delphi, where she would visit the site of the oracle and ask her burning question.

There were many more places in Greece that she

would have loved to visit—Thessaloniki, the home of Alexander the Great, the rock-hewn monasteries of Meteora, and especially the islands of Crete and Santorini—but they would have to wait for another trip. When she had studied Greek history, Julia had fallen in love with the sunny, carefree Minoan culture. She had pored over pictures of the colorful frescoes in blue and green and terra-cotta, of cavorting monkeys and dolphins, of wasp-waisted loinclothed men with headdresses of lilies, of acrobats somersaulting over the horns of a bull, of court ladies gowned in tiered skirts and embroidered boleros that bared their breasts. It seemed such a happy and fun-loving society. Julia would have loved to visit the Minoan archeological sites, but would have to content herself with viewing their artifacts in the national museum in Athens.

Her flight was being called. She boarded the plane and found her seat, then waited with fastened seat belt and unopened book for thirty minutes. She was always a bit nervous at takeoff and landing. Finally an announcement informed them of minor engine trouble. They were all to disembark. Her seatmate, a curly haired Greek with a too eager smile, insisted upon buying her a coffee at the bar and himself an ouzo. He displayed pictures of his family to establish his credentials and to allay any concerns she might have. He then asked where she would be traveling. When she told him her itinerary, he was clearly upset.

"You mean you are not visiting Crete, the cradle of Greek civilization? It is my home. I am a Cretan. I am Spyros Myrodopolis, architect. How can you not see the palace of Knossos?"

"I would love to—" she began.

"And Aghios Nickolaos, the town where I was born. A little fishing village with sandy beaches and herring fleets, sponge divers and tavernas right on the sea serving fish they catch that very hour."

"Sounds lovely," she said.

"It is magnificent," he proclaimed.

"Unfortunately, I only have two weeks," she explained.

"So you extend," the man insisted. "How many times do you come to Greece?"

"It's my first time," she admitted.

He raised his glass. "*Yassas.* You have much beauty awaiting you." Then he added gallantly, "And you bring much beauty with you."

Their flight was being called again. As they walked through the metal detecting stall, the buzzer went off loudly. When the uniformed guard approached, the architect smiled weakly. "It's my truss," he said. "I've got to have this hernia operated on."

Six hours later, the hernia prevented him from

helping her wrestle her bag off the conveyor belt in Athens, and he was involved in hailing a cab when she dragged her heavy suitcase across the dusty street to the airport bus. So much for courtliness, she thought.

The bus let her off a block from her hotel. She had booked the Astir online. It was well-located, air-conditioned and in the right price range. Now that Greece had changed its currency to the euro, hotel rates had gone up astronomically. The Astir was disappointing. Although the outside was serviceable, the inside was a disaster. It managed to be both unfinished and run-down at the same time; the elevators groaned and jerked, the air-conditioning was broken. Her room was tiny, the mattress lumpy, the pillow hard.

And worst of all, the hotel dining room was a windowless cave with fuzzy green walls and a listless ceiling fan. The only other guests were two elderly couples who slurped their soup and spat out their fish bones with noisy diligence.

Not exactly the romantic setting she had imagined, but her students would hardly notice, Julia hoped. They'd be busy all day and the only meal included was breakfast. She'd be darned if she would have her first meal in Athens in this dismal setting. Instead she headed out for the Plaka, its main square abuzz with lights and strolling people and inviting sidewalk cafés. She took a seat at an outdoor restaurant called Aphrodite, deeming it a good omen, and ordered a frosty Hellas beer.

She surveyed the menu and decided on stuffed grape leaves and a creamy moussaka. The waiter brought her a plate of purple olives and crusty bread and asked her where in America she was from. When she told him Los Angeles, he grinned broadly, showing several shiny gold teeth. "I live in Chicago for one year," he confided. "After work everyone go home. Close the door. Watch TV. I almost die of loneliness. In Greece we go to the taverna, meet our friends, drink, dance, laugh, make love. In America you live to work. In Greece we work to live."

Julia smiled in approval. After finishing every bit of her meal, she paid the bill and added a substantial tip. Life was what you made it. Bad hotel, lovely dinner, solicitous waiter, and tomorrow she would see Athens.

She slept well despite the minimal comforts of the room, and the morning coffee was surprisingly rich and fragrant. When she handed her room key to the desk clerk, he greeted her warmly and handed her a postcard and a message. The postcard was from Wendy, carefully mailed weeks ago. It was a picture of a Disneyland Mickey and Minnie Mouse and on the back Wendy had written in large block letters, "I MISS YOU. DO YOU MISS ME? YOUR DAUGHTER." Julia grinned and tucked the card into her purse. The message was from a Mr. Vasilius, their travel representative, who would meet her at the airport to greet the arriving students.

Mr. Vasilius turned out to be a short, chubby, effusive man who, true to his word, met her at the arrival gate sporting a large sign, "Welcome Los Angeles Community College."

The girls got off first, toting backpacks and carry-ons, looking rumpled and dazed. Behind them came Michael, tall and straight, his perpetual tan set off by a white linen jacket. His dark eyes scanned the crowd, alighted on her, squinted slightly to focus, then a slow smile of greeting. He held out his arms for a hug and drew her surprisingly close, until her breasts were pressed against his muscular chest. She felt enveloped by him, his scent, his sinew. She pulled back a bit. "Hi... there," she stammered. "Welcome to Greece."

"Great to see you," he said. "You're looking very well."

She could feel the color rise in her cheeks. It was going to be fun spending time with Michael, a lovely bonus. She pointed the way to passport control. He thanked her and moved toward the rapidly growing line.

It was then that she saw Sabrina, waiting a few feet away. Sabrina looked young and fresh in cutoff jeans and a midriff-revealing red spandex T-shirt. "How was the flight?" Julia asked.

"Traumatic," Sabrina said with a laugh. "A two hour delay, then they ran out of booze halfway here, but we managed to survive. Everybody made it except Alice Henderson. She's having an abortion, thank you very much, and won't be joining us." Sabrina arched her bra-less chest in a sensuous feline ripple. "So where do I go now?"

Julia pointed to the passport line and watched while Sabrina, after a moment's surveillance of the queue, glided up to Michael and with a graceful little hand gesture, slipped into place in front of him. Something in the angle of the girl's head, in the sway of her hips, in the closeness of the two bodies set off a warning bell in Julia. She had a strong intimation that in her absence, an agreement had been made, and she would be a reluctant and pained witness to its unfolding.

4

Julia's intimation proved correct, and the scenario played out in even worse ways than she had imagined. The two weeks had been interminable, but the trip was finally over. They were back at the Athens airport, which was buzzing with flies, with languages, with sweating tourists banging their heavy scuffed suitcases against each other's shins. Julia stood before the Olympic Airways counter with a smiling Mr. Vasilius, their Greek tour representative. He had been smiling when he met the group, but today the smile seemed truly genuine. He was divesting himself of the responsibility for twenty-nine college girls, three chaperones and dozens of problems, most dealing with loss—lost suitcases, lost passports, lost traveler's checks. Now he was tucking sixty baggage stubs in her right hand and a clutch of boarding passes, airline receipts, passports and custom declaration forms in her left. In lieu of a handshake, he bowed profusely and made a hasty exit.

Julia made her way to the airport café where she had instructed the group to wait. She stood in the center of the noisy room and began calling the girls' names. Few came to claim their documents. Maybe they couldn't hear. Maybe they were drinking cold Hellas beer or shopping for last minute souvenirs. Her eye caught Sabrina's. The girl gave her a stolid stare. Things had indeed deteriorated between them. Julia felt a quick stab of anger, tempered by a faint wash of guilt. She set her mouth and spoke evenly. "Sabrina, would you take half of these and distribute them, please?" The "please" stuck in her throat.

The girl rose languidly and snaked her way forward, a motion indicating that Michael was within eye range. And he was, slumped in a seat, fanning himself with an airmail edition of the *Herald Tribune*. Was he gazing at Sabrina with that familiar half-lidded look of desire? No, his eyes were on the floor. He seemed ill. He had a cold. Too bad, Julia thought. Let him drown in his own secretions.

The trip had been a torment. Her nerves were taut as wire; her pants gaped about her waist from the weight she'd lost and her pallor showed yellow beneath her tan.

The documents distributed, several of the girls extending their vacation in Greece came up to say goodbye, as did Sabrina, who was going on to Mykonos and Corfu. "See you in a few weeks," Sabrina said, executing a game little wave, stubborn to the end.

Julia pretended not to see it, just as she pretended not to see Michael approach, although she had clocked his movement from his first step. She imagined several choice scenarios as she waited for him to speak. Hangdog… "I'm sorry, Julia, I was a fool." Cavalier… "Well, Sabrina and I were both single and Greece is an aphrodisiac." Conciliatory… "Let me have your boarding pass, I'll make sure our seats are together. We can catch up." Instead he spoke in a gravelly monotone. "Julia, could you please see about getting me an aisle seat? I must have a touch of the flu."

And instead of suggesting that he speak to the flight attendant himself, she found herself taking his boarding pass and explaining the situation to the service representative just as if she were a tour guide instead of a university professor and then returning with a new seat assignment.

"Thaaank you," he said, with that extended vowel actors have, and sat down, closing his eyes.

The end of a chapter, a melodrama, a farce, a teaching tale. Moral: beware of your dreams. They might come true and haunt you. Indeed, the whole study tour had begun with a daydream of swimming in the wine-dark Aegean with Michael Carpenter. Her mistake had been to enlist the services of Sabrina. Months ago in the planning stages, when she had told Sabrina that Michael would be coming along, would need a single accommodation as the only man, Sabrina had dimpled and said, "Michael Carpenter, he can always room with me." Prophetic? Calculated? Accomplished nightly. The knowledge of it twisted like a knife in Julia's belly.

This was her payment for bringing him to Greece. This was the conclusion to a three-year friendship. The times when she had brought him on the campus to lecture and to guest direct he had seemed so friendly, so interested in her. The way he had taken her arm as they crossed the street. The way he had touched her shoulder to make a point. The warm conspiratorial smiles. Hadn't those been messages? Or had she just imagined they were? She was married. She wasn't looking for a love affair, only a friendship, a mild flirtation. A safe, controlled interaction that would act as a sweet extra to a wonderful trip. Greece would provide the time and space for a leisurely small adventure.

But Greece turned out to provide something far different. How could he prefer Sabrina to her? Sabrina was an immature, self-involved airhead…who also happened to be younger, prettier and sexually available. Oh, hell, Julia thought, I have wit and compassion. I've borne and raised two children. I've got Mediterranean skin that doesn't wrinkle and I'm much more interesting than I was at twenty. But still Michael had chosen Sabrina.

So it was not to be, that imagined flirtation in an exotic locale. Memories she could take home to feed her bedtime fantasies. She had been rigorously faithful for twenty years, although in the last few years it had become more difficult. Anything could trigger her longings—a romantic movie, a love song, a couple kissing. Sometimes she could bury her desire for months, bank the fire in her blood, but it was like chilling the body for heart surgery, useful only for a time or she would die of the cold.

She had laboriously engineered the trip to Greece, pulled strings for it and made sure that Michael was onboard. And that first night together in Athens everything seemed to be working beautifully. She had bought two tickets to the performance of *Oedipus at Colonnos* at the Herod Atticus, the ancient stone amphitheater under the stars. Just the two of them, the tragic tale, the barefooted toga-clad actors, the sibilant cries of the Greek chorus. Then dinner *à deux* at a rooftop restaurant— they'd shared peppery scampi, sweet pink melon, an icy carafe of dry white wine. The conversation was animated, mutual, with easy segues, lots of laughter. So different from the obligatory, mundane conversations that she had with Mark. As she sipped her espresso she'd reflected, with a bit of guilt, that perhaps all marital exchanges devolved to that familiar comfort level. It was not unusual that the new and the novel sparked interest.

When the bill came and Michael reached for it, Julia insisted upon splitting it. That made it much more of an evening with a colleague, she reasoned, rather than a date. But in the taxi ride back to the hotel, Michael sat close to her, their shoulders brushing. She could feel the warmth of his body through his thin shirt but she didn't move away. Instead she kept up a running conversation about the ancient monuments they were passing, the wonders of Athens. She could sense his desire but was afraid to turn toward him, to lift her mouth for his kiss. She had fallen asleep many nights the last few weeks fantasizing about such a kiss. Suddenly she felt Michael's arm around her shoulder, drawing her to him.

His mouth pressed against hers, determined and lustful. She kissed back, flushed and breathless, yet strangely unmoved. His desire felt hasty, impersonal. Where was the tenderness, the wonder?

As they exited the cab and entered the hotel lobby, she quickly surveyed the space to see if any of the girls or Sabrina were there. She was relieved that they weren't. Not that anything untoward had happened, but still, appearances were important. She had a position to maintain. In the elevator, Michael asked her floor number, and when they arrived, followed her out.

"Are you on the same floor?" she asked naively, knowing he wasn't.

"No, just thought I'd see you to your door," he replied.

"That's very gentlemanly of you," she said, smiling.

"I had a great time. Do you want to invite me in?"

"It's pretty late," she demurred.

"Not for Greece," he countered.

As she fumbled for her key, he pulled her toward him, his mouth on hers, his body full against hers, pressing hard. She drew back.

"What's wrong?" he asked.

It's too soon, she thought. It doesn't feel right. "I think we've had too much wine," she said, attempting levity.

He pulled away immediately. "Sorry. I didn't mean to upset you. See you tomorrow." He made a hasty retreat to the elevator.

She had trouble sleeping that night. Her body was aroused by the contact, her mind unsettled. She knew she had made the right decision. That wasn't what she had wanted. And yet…

That next morning at the Parthenon, he had found Sabrina. Each time Julia turned to look at Michael he was standing so near the girl that the hairs on their arms bristled. Julia could feel the electricity. That afternoon, when the rest of the group returned to the hotel, they did not. That evening one of the students blurted, "Hey, Mrs. Simon, Sabrina said Michael took her to a great beach. Vouligmeni. Can we go? She says it's not crowded at all."

There was the beginning salvo of two weeks of feeling the heat between them. They were discreet—never an overt touch or endearment, but the space between them was charged. Night after night at the group dinners, when the Greek air was liquid and fragrant as Hymettus honey and the stars blazed in the blue-back sky, Julia was witness to the courtship dance between them, the lingering meeting of the eyes, the private smiles. And, of course, she spent very little time with Michael. Even when they would find themselves sitting next to each other on the bus or at a site, his conversation was perfunctory and his attention was elsewhere, his eyes roaming, scouting for Sabrina.

The girl herself was useless. One night the group had dined at the Sounion Peninsula overlooking the glistening marble pillars of the Temple of Dionysius, the god of wine, of inspiration, of the irrational. Julia had returned to her hotel room and realized that she had misplaced her itinerary and needed to know the starting time for tomorrow. She'd dialed Sabrina's room. The phone rang and rang. It was well after midnight and no one was there. Perversely, unable to stop, she phoned every twenty minutes until almost dawn. It was just self-torture; she knew Sabrina must be in Michael's bed, lost in the deep sleep that follows vigorous and satisfying lovemaking.

And theirs wasn't the only romance; many of the girls made their own liaisons among the guides, the drivers, the waiters in the tavernas, the local boys in their tight black trousers and embroidered shirts. Julia watched as the girls were swept up in strong male arms and introduced to the hypnotic rhythms of the Greek circle dances, and afterward led to a walk on the beach to listen to the song of the Aegean as it caressed the ancient stones. Greece was the epitome of romance. The birthplace of Eros. You had to be dead not to feel it. And Julia felt that restlessness, that longing intensify as the trip wore on. She couldn't wait for it to be over, to be freed from observing Sabrina and Michael.

Finally they reached their last destination, Delphi. The sanctuary was nestled in a grove of olive and cypress trees, backed by the gleaming cliffs of Mount Parnassus. The girls settled on the stone steps of the Temple of Apollo and Julia explained the background and history of the sacred site. She was a good lecturer and her students paid close attention.

"Apollo's shrine at Delphi is the most famous oracle of antiquity," she explained. "Homer mentions it in the *Iliad*, but there it was called Pytho, named after an older goddess cult that was usurped by the advent of the male gods."

The girls hissed in disapproval. Apparently, they found no conflict between their dedication to feminism and their dalliance with handsome Greek waiters.

"The site was said to be discovered by chance," she continued, "when a shepherd noticed that his flock went into a frenzy anytime it came near a certain chasm in the rock. When he approached he also came under a spell by the emanations and began to utter prophecies, as did his fellow villagers."

Several of the girls grinned, and whispered among themselves about weed and magic mushrooms.

"It is said that the villagers chose a woman from among their midst to sit over the chasm on a three-footed stool and to prophesy. This woman, the Pythia, was always middle-aged, and upon her appointment had to give up normal life and live in seclusion. On oracle days, the seventh of the month..." Julia paused and noted that today was the seventh of June. No accident, that. She had arranged it that way. The girls exclaimed in wonder, impressed. "...the Pythia would then enter into the temple of Apollo, sit on the tripod and drink the Castillian water."

Julia pointed in the direction of the Castillian Spring below the temple, where clear water still ran. "The oracle would then fall into a trance and answer the questions that were posed to her. Citizens would line up for days to consult her. Animal sacrifices were made and gifts given. For the oracle spoke directly from the gods and could predict the future. Her proclamations were never literal, though, always equivocal, always open to interpretation."

Julia concluded the talk by recounting the most famous of the sibylline answers. It was given to King Croesus of Lydia, who asked if he should attack the Persians. "Croesus, having crossed the Halys River, will destroy a great realm," the Pythia said. Encouraged, Croesus crossed the river, fought the Persians and lost. The Pythia was right, but it was his *own* realm that was destroyed.

"You're free to explore the site on your own," Julia said. "Ask those questions you want guidance for, and who knows, you may get some answers. At least from your own inner wisdom." There was a smattering of appreciative applause as the girls scattered, most heading down to the Castillian spring. Despite herself, Julia tracked the movement of Michael and Sabrina as they wandered off together.

She waited until everyone had dispersed and she was sure she was alone. She cleansed her hands and mouth in the Castillian water and sat close to the opening in the rock, hands folded, eyes shut, and silently asked her question. The question she had flown three thousand miles to ask.

And as she sat in meditation, an answer came. Properly equivocal, but she heard it clearly: *Water the roots*. She knew she wasn't imagining it. She doubted if she was fabricating it. It seemed to come from a deeper source, perhaps from her inner wisewoman, as she'd suggested to the girls. But what roots? The roots of her own personality? The roots of her desire? The roots of her marriage and family? It seemed to echo her mother's parting words: "Live, Julia. Live." But how? How to reconcile her own needs and everyone else's? This longing for love? For growth? For change? What to listen to? Whom to trust?

"United Airlines Flight 840 for San Francisco now available for boarding at gate 2." Here, at the Athens airport on the day of her departure from Greece, the question still haunted her. The hoped-for answer was as elusive as ever.

Julia hoisted her purse a bit more securely upon her shoulder and strode ahead, arms swinging freely. It was a source of pride not to be encumbered with carry-on baggage, to be able to thread her way with ease through the crowd, a free spirit not given to rank conspicuous consumption. Behind her, she caught a glimpse of two of her golden-haired charges struggling with camera bags, statuary, vases and rolled up flokati rugs. She chose to ignore them, neither to shoulder a bag herself nor aid in finding a cart. They were adults, they had their tickets, they could cope. Two weeks of babysitting twenty-nine charges was enough, mediating their complaints to chambermaids and desk clerks, doling out aspirin and Lomotil, lending stamps, translating euros into dollars, softening quarrels, counting heads, dining with the undesirables, exclaiming over the purchase of garish shirts already beginning to shred at the seams.

She walked quickly, arriving at the gate to find a seething mass of screaming babies, black-clad matrons, darting Greek men in tight bottomed pants, all pushing against each other, fearful that there would not be enough seats despite the numbered boarding passes. She circled back, saw a deserted door near the rear of the runway and made for it. Gratefully, she breathed in the wisps of fresh air and looked back. Her own entourage had joined the press at the glass. She was alone except for a man to her left. She appraised him with a sideward glance. Thirtyish, with luxuriant red-gold hair and beard, broad shoulders shown to advantage in a thin embroidered shirt. He was carrying a large, black leather case, heavily buckled and strapped. Although she felt his own appraising glance, she kept her eyes on the approaching plane. But now the space between them had dimensions. It felt good to be noticed after weeks of near invisibility.

The plane taxied in. She and the red-haired man stood waiting in silence, watching the nearby crowd surge in their glass cage, when surprisingly, a boarding platform lowered from the rear of the plane and a flight attendant beckoned them aboard. As they headed across the asphalt, they fell into step together. He grinned, revealing a boyish overbite that lent a note of playfulness to his strong mobile face.

"Lucked out," he said, pointing over his shoulder; the other door had just opened, and people were pushing so hard they blocked the doorway.

She nodded conspiratorially. Glancing at the massive leather case bumping against his thigh, she asked, "What's in there?"

"Treasure."

"Pirate's treasure?" she asked.

"Greek treasure from Thera. Did you get there?"

"Thera?" she said. "I don't think so."

"The modern name is Santorini."

"Oh, no, I didn't. I would have loved it, though. Especially the excavations."

"Well, you're in luck," he said with a grin. "We've found some wonderful things. If you're interested, I've brought some slides."

"You're connected to the excavation?"

"Head of the underwater team," he said. "Where are you sitting?"

She showed him her seat stub.

"I'm in Nineteen G and I've bought an extra seat for my box," he said.

"That's extravagant," she said.

"It's too big for the overhead compartment. And I won't let it out of my sight. Come and sit with me. I'll put it on the floor."

"I'm sorry, but I can't. I'm with a group of students."

"That group you were handing out tickets to? They're old enough to handle a plane ride alone. And anyway, they can't get lost, there's nowhere to go. My name's Ted. Nineteen G. Got it?" He grazed her arm in parting. She felt the touch all the way to her seat. So simple. A brief conversation and this perfectly attractive man had suggested she sit next to him. He had invited her. Just like that.

She made her way to her seat. It was a vast plane—ten seats across. Her students hadn't arrived yet. She sat quietly, smiling, her first easy smile in two weeks. She checked her face in her mirrored compact and noticed her lower lip was blistered with a cold sore. Herpes simplex, a sign of stress. She dabbed at it with a tissue. An ill omen, she thought, like a pimple before the prom. The business with Michael had detonated her ego. She checked her hair in the mirror. It shone black with auburn highlights, long and soft on her shoulders. She noticed as she parted it down the middle, though, that the gray roots showed. It needed a touch-up. She combed it straight back, fluffing the top layer to conceal the roots. He was younger, she was sure. Ten years, perhaps. Why was she even thinking of that? she chided herself. Never mind, she concluded. She was genuinely interested in Santorini and it would be good therapy to talk to a man who wasn't looking over her shoulder for someone else.

The plane began to fill with tour members. Francine, the myopic poet with the apologetic cough, sat on one side of Julia and Hippolyta, the self-styled astrologer, wafting clouds of patchouli oil, sat on the other. The voice of a flight attendant blasted through the cabin. "Fasten your seat belts, place all seat backs and tray tables in an upright position for takeoff." Farewell Greece, Julia thought, farewell unrequited dream.

On her left, Francine read the poems of Sappho. On her right, Hippolyta pored over the cache of miniature, double-bladed axes she had bought for her San Francisco coven, and offered to read Julia's tarot. The wonders of

California's alternative cultures, Julia thought. Other members drifted up the aisle, wanting to know about the length of the final paper, and how to get a refund for not getting a single room. Did she know the custom regulations? Did she have any aspirin?

Julia quickly answered their questions, then closed her unread *New Yorker*, unsnapped her seat belt and made her way up the aisle. She passed Michael's blanketed form slouched in his seat. She could stop, inquire about his health, bring him some juice. He looked pale. Too bad, she thought, and walked on. That chapter was over.

Ted was sitting in the next section of the plane, front row aisle, his massive black case resting on the seat beside him. He looked up as she neared, smiled with genuine welcome and stowed the box carefully on the floor. "I'm glad you came…." He trailed off, discovering he did not know her name.

"Julia," she offered. "I can't stay long. I'll have to get back in a minute." She squeezed past him and into the empty seat.

"Why?"

"There are things to be done," she said, trying to think of some reason why she shouldn't stay.

"On an airplane?"

"Well, I am responsible, you know. It's my job."

"It's time for a break." He signaled a passing attendant. "Champagne, please."

"At nine in the morning?" Julia asked.

"It's cocktail time in San Francisco." When the bottle arrived, he poured the bubbling liquid into two plastic glasses. As she took one, he clinked his against it. "To a shared journey," he said. A charming and intriguingly ambiguous toast.

She took a deep drink of the champagne. It was tingling and tangy on her lips, then icy cold as it ran down her chin. The plastic glass had split, sending a rivulet down the front of her blouse and forming a puddle in her lap.

"Oops," he said, helping her to wipe up the spill and then signaling for a new glass.

"It's okay," she said. "It's a metaphor for the last few weeks."

"That bad, eh?" he asked.

"Professionally it was a success. Personally it was a disaster. At any rate, I don't want to talk about it." She looked down at the front of her blouse; the champagne had wet through to her bra, highlighting her nipple like a button on a doorbell. She shrugged. What the hell, Sabrina had dispensed with bras entirely. Julia tilted her seat back and sipped the replacement champagne he had poured. "Tell me all about your expedition," she said.

And as they drank their champagne, he did. He was a classical archeologist and had spent the last four summers excavating in Akrotiri. He extracted a box of slides from his jacket pocket. Holding them up to the light of the window, he explained their contents, one by one, as she peered at them. They had all been found in this season's dig, he said, not yet published or exhibited. They revealed a bronze dagger engraved with the royal sign of the double-bladed ax, a storage jar painted with swirling octopuses and starfish, and a splendid fresco of the bull dance, a twin to the one at Knossos.

As he spoke, she studied the expressive curve of his mouth ringed by the luxuriant bronze of his beard, watched the play of light in his startlingly green eyes, how his brows drew together when he searched for a phrase, and spread like wings when he found it. His words were like subtitles in a foreign movie; the feeling and meaning lay in his face, in his gestures. She listened and was absorbed.

This summer, he told her with growing excitement, he had finally found what he had been looking for. Concrete evidence of what he had long suspected—that the remains of the lost Atlantis were buried underwater in the center of the caldera, the volcanic lake, on Thera. He told her of the first mention of the island utopia in Plato's *Critias* and how ever since, mankind had been searching for the famed Atlantis, the golden island that had disappeared in a day and a night. Now all the evidence from geology, seismology, vulcanology, archeology pointed to Thera as the historical site of the fabled civilization. Thera was the religious capital and Crete, its larger neighboring island, the city-state of a brilliant Minoan civilization that had dominated the Mediterranean and was destroyed in 1500 B.C. by a devastating volcanic eruption, just as Plato had written.

In the center of the collapsed caldera of the volcano, under water half a mile deep, he was certain lay the site of the Temple of Poseidon. Plato had described it as a splendid structure of hammered silver and gold, with an ivory roof, and inside it was one of the wonders of the ancient world—a thirty-foot statue of Poseidon made of gold, standing on a golden chariot with six winged horses. Julia watched Ted's face glow with excitement, his eyes like fireflies. "It's there under the sea. The seismograph and magnetograph readings prove it. It'll cost a fortune to dredge but it's worth it. Schleimann found Troy with a spade and a copy of the *Iliad*. Nobody believed him, either, said it was myth, a fantasy. But it was real. And so is this." He took a deep breath. "I'm talking too much. Let's have some more champagne."

"I don't know if I should." She hesitated.

"You're not driving, are you?" he joked, placing his

hand on hers. His touch felt wonderful, like slipping on a fur-lined mitten on a snowy day. The warmth spread through her body, thawing the icy places with almost audible cracks.

When the champagne came, he once again clinked his glass against hers. "Careful," she cautioned, "remember what happened last time."

"Not to worry," he said with a smile. "I like cleaning it up." He checked his watch. "Nine hours to go. Lucky us."

She nodded, her thoughts exactly. It was a rare treat to encounter such an interesting and interested man. She saw Francine come up the aisle, studiously casual. Then, with feigned surprise, the student said, "Mrs. Simon, I wondered what happened to you."

Julia shifted in her seat, straightening her spine. She noticed how Ted's eyes followed her movements.

A quick memory flashed, of how hard she had tried to lure Michael's glance and failed. That first night, she had worn a white clinging dress that highlighted the copper of her skin. Michael had done a theatrical take. "What a beauty," he had said. But the next day, when he was fixated on Sabrina's bare thighs and gauzy halters, Julia had felt as unappealing as a third helping of baklava. The less he had noticed her, the more carefully she had dressed and posed and preened. Needing to know she was still attractive. Still appealing. All to no avail.

And now, with no effort on her part at all, this new man was fully attentive, fully engaged. He looked at her with pleasure, listened eagerly to what she said, laughed at her jokes. It was only when she felt her jaws soften and relax that she realized that she had been clenching her teeth. For how long? A tightness melted from her cheeks and the corners of her eyes. She met his gaze fully.

"Hey," he said, "that's better."

"What is?"

"You know what I mean."

She nodded. "I guess I was pretty tense."

"Welcome to the here and now."

The flight attendant came round with lunch menus, Chicken Hawaiian or Beef Burgundy, and a tangle of earphones.

"Want to watch the movie?" Julia asked as she accepted a pair of earphones.

Ted shook his head. "We don't need those. We can entertain each other. All right if I lift this?" He raised the armrest that separated them. "It'll give us more room."

Julia felt her breath catch. What was this all about? She stowed her earphones in her seat pocket. "Tell me more about Thera," she said.

Expertly, with darting words, he painted the wonders of the Minoan civilization, the seagoing triremes, the hydraulic engineering, the bull dancers, the court ladies with their bare breasts and girdled waists. Then he talked of himself, of his stint as a tuna fisherman, of how he had raced motorcycles until he had broken more bones than he could count, of how he had studied poetry at the New School. At her request, he recited the first poem he had written, "The Eskimos have seventeen words for snow. My fingers have walked the valleys of your thighs. I know there are more."

He told her of Ann, an archeologist girlfriend, who was on a dig somewhere in Turkey. They'd had an on-again, off-again relationship since graduate school. But it was when he talked of the upcoming conference in San Francisco to which he was heading that his voice raced with excitement. "It could be the most important event in my life," he said. "A chance to prove that Thera is truly Atlantis, and hidden in its caldera, a mile beneath the sea, is its crowning monument, the Temple of Poseidon. It could make archeological history, international head-lines, as big as Mycenae, as Thebes, as Pompeii. And I have the evidence to prove it right here."

"You have the evidence in that case?" she asked, sur-prised. "What is it?"

"You'll have to wait for that," he teased. "Now it's your turn. I want to hear all about you."

She started with the most recent event and told him

about the trip, about the visit to Delphi and its Oracle, the lectures she'd given and then briefly about the affair between Michael and Sabrina. "It made the trip a bit lonely," she said, "not having adult company or an assistant." She edited out her own unfulfilled romantic longings.

"They did a number on you, all right," he said, "but you can't legislate affection." In his dispassionate appraisal, her disappointment assumed the proportions of a paper cut, a fiery, momentary stinging, neither deep nor vital.

"Married?" he asked, indicating her wedding ring.

"Yes," she said.

"Happily?"

"Twenty years."

He raised a quizzical eyebrow. "Children?" he asked.

"Two. Wendy and Davey. They're great kids."

Then she talked about her job and the last seminar she had taught on Beckett. Ted knew *Godot* but not *Endgame*, the later, darker play. She paused to describe the curious relationship of the characters of Hamm and Clove, who might be lovers, father and son, master and servant. And then, flushed with the drink, she recited her favorite passage for him: "'Hamm says that once he knew a madman who thought the end of the world had come. Hamm used to go and see him in the asylum, take him by the hand and drag him to the window, make him look at the rising corn, the sails of the herring fleet! All that loveliness! But the other man would just pull his hand away and go back into his corner. Appalled. To him all was ashes. It appears the case is…was not so…so unusual.'"

Ted listened, entranced. "Yes, I believe that. We create our own reality. Recite more," he said softly, "it's wonderful." But she colored beneath the intensity of his gaze, for the piece summoned a memory that threatened to spill into speech, the time of her own depression. Instead, she attempted to switch the conversation to a safer place.

But Ted caught the change of her expression. "So what is it you don't want to tell me?" he asked.

"Just a little dark night of the soul," she confessed. "We can talk about it later." She touched his hand in gratitude for his concern. "Hey," she said, pointing to the space between his thumb and first finger, "you're a tennis player."

"Excellent sleuthing, Sherlock," he declared with a grin.

"That muscle always gets developed. It's where you grip the racket." She displayed her own tennis muscle. "I even brought my racket. Too bad we didn't meet before. We could have had a game."

"Never too late," he said.

The movie screens rolled down and colored images flashed overhead. All around them people adjusted seats, fumbled with earphones. "If we're lucky, they'll turn out the lights," Ted said.

She smiled in agreement; they were as visible as teenagers on the family couch. Their seats were directly in front of the bathrooms, and the girls had the bladder capacity of kittens.

But as the hours went on, decorum mattered less than the growing warmth between the two of them They gravitated toward each other easily, like a tropism. It wasn't so much that Julia sought the physical contact, it was more that when it happened she didn't move away. In between the girls' surveillances, she and Ted sat with thighs and shoulders discreetly touching. Their fingers brushed against each other as they shared sections of the *Athens News*. When Ted bent forward to extract a magazine from a forward pocket his hand gently grazed her knee.

When he rose to view Nova Scotia through the plane window, she appraised his body, admiring the breadth of his shoulders, his narrow hips and strong thighs. And when it was her turn to become vertical she tugged at the gaping waistband of her pants and complained of having lost weight, of being too thin. He appraised her from half-closed lids. "You are," he said slowly and deliberately, "just right."

She could feel a flush spread through her body from her scalp to her knees. She sank back into her seat, her eyes still meshed with his. These moments together were like pieces in a jigsaw puzzle, the disparate edges fitting, the colors blending to make a preordained shape. Her heart was beating fast. Her breath caught in her throat. She ran the tip of her tongue around her mouth.

"My lips are so dry," she murmured.

"Maybe I can help," he said. He leaned across and with moist open lips kissed her lightly on the mouth. It was inappropriate. Scandalous. But it felt wonderful.

"Oh," she sighed as they moved apart. "I really *needed* to meet you. I was in terrible shape."

"I didn't *need* to meet anyone," he said. "You just happened and now I want more."

"More?" she laughed. "We'd have to join the mile high club." She blushed, abashed at her own audacity. Blame it on the champagne.

He shook his head. "I want a big soft double bed and lots of time."

"I was just kidding," she demurred.

"I wasn't. Stay with me tonight."

"Stay…where?"

"In San Francisco."

"I'm expected in Los Angeles."

"What would happen if you were a day late?"

"They'd be worried. Mark and the children are meeting me at the airport."

"Call him and tell him you're delayed."

"I can't do that."

"Of course you can," he said. "Tell him you're sick."

"It would be a lie," she said.

"Then tell him the truth. That you've met someone you want to get to know better. What's a night or two, Julia? You were going to spend two weeks with Michael."

"But that was different. He was teaching on the program. And it was just a harmless flirtation."

"You don't have to decide just yet," he said smiling. "You've still got a few minutes."

Spend the night in San Francisco? The thought was both frightening and alluring. She had never been unfaithful to Mark and didn't intend to be. And yet wasn't Ted's invitation a fitting compensation for the frustrations she had endured in Greece?

A line from T. S. Eliot came to mind, "There will be time for a hundred indecisions and a hundred visions and revisions before the taking of toast and tea." The advantage of being an English teacher. There was always a relevant quote. Someone else's experience, exquisitely phrased, substituting for her own.

As if on cue, the Fasten Seat Belts sign flashed, confirmed by the loudspeaker. "We are making our descent into San Francisco International Airport. The weather is clear, visibility excellent."

Ted folded her hand in his. "We're safe from detection now, your charges are all buckled in." They sat silently as the big plane gradually lost altitude, opened its flaps, touched earth, then taxied slowly to the waiting ramp. They never moved, constant as the horizon, while all around them, despite the flight attendant's admonition to keep their seats until the plane came to a complete stop, passengers darted about retrieving possessions, struggling into coats, lining up in the aisles. A number of students threw Julia quizzical looks as they walked by, until finally Hippolyta queried sharply, "Aren't you getting off? You've got all the baggage stubs."

They stood then and made their way down the now deserted aisle, Ted carrying the black case, the contents of which, she realized, she still had not seen. They entered the terminal and made their way to baggage claim. She stood apart as Ted waited to retrieve their bags from the slowly moving belt. She turned, surprised by a gravelly voice at her shoulder. It was Michael.

"I seem to have lost my customs declaration," he explained. "Have you another?"

"I don't," she said, then quickly softened her curtness. "Why don't you ask the man in the blue uniform? He'll have one." Michael had become as dependent, as witless as the girls.

He smiled, took her hand in both of his. "*Thank* you," he said. "It was a good trip." A jaunty wave and he was off, fading into the crowd. She watched him go, surprised at how detached she felt. It was like watching the last frame of a B movie. Where had it gone, that attraction, that desire? How could she have transferred it so neatly, in the space of a day, to another man? Was it all an illusion? Simple projection? Yet the longings were real. Then and now. That she knew. What she needed to find out was what generated those feelings. And where should they be placed.

Ted retrieved her suitcase and they joined the customs line. All around them students scurried about with rolling carts, embracing each other in hurried goodbyes and racing to connecting flights. Julia and Ted stood outside the customs gate, hands burdened with luggage, yet still leaning in, held in a gravitational field, eyes locked, mouths set and grim. She was connected to him. To move away would be wrenching. There was something still unexplored, something important.

She forced herself to take a step back, to hold out her hand. "You've got my office e-mail and phone number. We'll keep in touch."

He took her outstretched palm and pressed it to his

mouth. She felt the flick of his warm tongue circling. "You'll be home tomorrow in time for dinner," he promised. She felt her knees weaken, a sunburst of heat at her groin.

"I can't, Ted. I really can't," she protested.

"You need to do something nice for yourself. A weekend to recoup. And don't you want to know what I've got in my big black box?"

"Yes, of course I do. Tell me."

"You've got to come to the conference and find out."

"Tease," she berated him.

"You'll be my guest," he continued. "I've booked an extra room for my dive master, but he couldn't make it. You can have his room. All on the up-and-up. And the conference will be useful to you. Classical archeology. You can use the material for your Greek tragedy course. Think of the benefit to your students. Especially for that junior witch, the one with the double-bladed ax. Wait till she presents my findings to her coven."

"I can't," Julia reiterated, but her protest was lessening.

"I asked you if you were happily married. You answered, 'Twenty years.' That wasn't very convincing."

"We're going through a bad patch," she admitted.

"Look, Julia, you didn't get your answer at Delphi. Maybe you can find it here." And with that, he tucked her arm firmly in his, and Julia found herself walking beside him out to queue of waiting taxis. She watched as Ted loaded their suitcases into the trunk of a cab. It was an extension of the same unreality that had begun in Athens when they had met at the airport. The same easy synchronicity. As if it were fated. Something important was presenting itself and she was helpless to refuse it. She took her seat in the taxi, staring out the window as couples and families embraced in sanctioned welcomes, while she herself was bound to Ted, a stranger, carried like a twig on the current of a river, only the river was within.

"It's going to be nice," he said as he settled beside her. His arm rested lightly around her shoulders like a feather boa, soft and warm and extravagantly out of place.

5

It was forty dollars by the taxi meter to the Saint Francis Hotel on Union Square. The fare had gone up since she and Mark had been there two years ago. While Ted registered for both rooms at the front desk, Julia found a phone booth to call Mark's office. She misdialed the first time, forgetting the familiar number, had to check her address book and dial again.

Mark's nurse answered, and instantly recognized her voice. "Dr. Simon, it's your wife," she called. Mark would always take Julia's phone calls, even in the midst of seeing a patient.

"Julia, how are you?" His voice was energetic, excited. "How was the trip?"

"It was fine. Everything went well," she said. "How are things at home?"

"Okay. We managed. Where are you?" he asked.

"San Francisco."

"When do you get into L.A.?"

Through the glass she could see Ted approaching. She watched him stride across the lobby toward her. He stood outside the booth, raised his hand to mirror hers where it pressed against the glass.

"What time is your plane?" Mark repeated. "We must have a bad connection, I can barely hear you." A bad connection—the common phrase seemed charged, diagnostic, prophetic.

"Mark, listen, I want to spend the night in San Francisco."

"Why?" he asked.

"There's a conference I want to attend."

"What kind of conference?"

"It's about Greek archeology. It'll be helpful for my theater course."

"But you're due home. The kids are expecting you. I'm expecting you."

"It's just one more day. I'll be home tomorrow."

"You never told me anything about a conference," he said accusingly.

"I just found out about it," she said. "And I'm here anyway." Then she added softly, "Okay?" If he said something gentle, something loving, if he said he missed her, needed her, she would take the next plane home. But instead, his voice was harsh and cold. "Listen to me, Julia. Stop the nonsense. I want you to come home. Now."

It was the tone of command, the harsh authoritarian fist banging on the table. She heard her father's voice when she was a child: "Why? Because I said so. That's why." And in it the echo of all the struggles that she and Mark had had, of every battle for independence, for self-hood. Her own anger and pride rose up against that familiar ultimatum. "I'm sorry," she said, "but I need to stay."

"When *will* you be home?" His voice bristled with anger.

"I'm not sure yet."

"Then how do you expect me to pick you up?"

"It's okay. I'll take a cab home."

"Suit yourself," he snapped. "You've been away two weeks. But that's not enough for you. Remind me not to be so agreeable next time."

She longed to remind him of all the medical conferences, golfing vacations, all those times she stayed at home with the children. But instead she said goodbye and hung up the phone. She rested her head against the wall and closed her eyes.

"Tough?" Ted asked.

She nodded.

"First time you told him no?"

"Not really, but this time it seems more important."

"I certainly hope so." He waved away the bellboy and hoisted their suitcases, and they rode the elevator to the eighth floor. Ted had arranged for adjacent rooms. He handed her the plastic card that opened her door.

"Can you be ready in half an hour?" he asked.

"Ready for what?"

"We're going to paint the town red before you go back to Kansas, Dorothy. Meet you at the bar in the lobby."

"What shall I wear?" she asked.

"Something festive," he said as he disappeared into his own room.

Julia's room was large and airy, with a Provençal decor, thick carpeting and lush draperies. The picture windows afforded a sweeping view of Union Square. The bathroom was gleaming marble and the tub boasted a Jacuzzi. It was definitely upmarket from the Greek hotels she had just frequented. Drawing herself a luxuriant bath, she scented the water with the complimentary lavender salts. She thought of her mother's gift of lavender perfume and wondered how her mom and dad were doing. She had called a few times from Greece and things were unchanged. She would call again first thing tomorrow, when she returned home.

But for now, she tuned the radio to classical FM and let the hot water soak away the residual aches and tightness from the long plane ride. She willed away any anxiety or doubts she had of the upcoming evening. Instead she recalled the Chinese pictogram for accident—two interlocking symbols, crisis and opportunity.

Clad in a plush terry-cloth robe, Julia opened her suitcase and surveyed her wardrobe. She could iron her blue linen pantsuit or rely on a serviceable black skirt and sweater. Neither was by any stretch of the imagination "festive." Indeed, there was only one item of clothing that fit the bill. One night in Olympus, egged on by the students and Sabrina's example, she had bought a long wraparound skirt and halter top of blue-and-white gauzy Greek cotton. The thin cloth revealed the outline of her body, the roundness of her breasts and thighs. It wasn't really suitable for San Francisco's urban scene and chilly winds, but it made her feel sensual, feminine. And she did have an all-purpose jacket that could be added for warmth and decorum.

Julia dabbed perfume on her wrists and neck, applied more makeup than usual: red lipstick and blush, midnight-blue mascara and liner. She added a pair of oversize gold hoop earrings and appraised herself in the mirror. Quite a transformation. No longer the college prof nor a soccer mom, but a wannabe gypsy dressed for a night on the town.

She barely recognized herself. Who was this new person? She was suddenly assailed by a wave of doubt, of misgiving, of guilt. She could still call the evening off, plead fatigue. She knew so little of Ted, really. And yet, she felt so alive, so excited, so curious. She had already made her excuses to Mark and it was just this one adventurous evening, she told herself. It would be a pity to lose courage now. She took a deep breath and headed for the bar.

As she strode across the lobby, Julia could feel the stir of interest she created, sense the admiring glances of men. Ted's smile was equally appreciative as she approached his table. "You look like a Greek goddess," he said. When he stood up to greet her, resplendent in a Greek wedding shirt of pleated muslin, she returned the compliment. "And you look like Odysseus."

He summoned the waitress and ordered two flutes of champagne. When they arrived, he toasted her. "To our own Odyssey."

She lifted her glass, but was looking reflexively around the room, scanning for a familiar face. What if someone she knew was there? She mentally rehearsed her story. Ted was a professional colleague; she was interested in his paper on Atlantis. They had met in Athens, and since she was going to be in San Francisco anyway... And Mark was just fine, thank you. She was going home tomorrow.

"Julia," Ted said, calling her back to the present moment. "You know what the Greeks say about toasts? If you don't make eye contact it's seven years of bad sex."

"Oh no!" she gasped in mock horror. "I wouldn't wish that on anyone." She held his gaze for a long intense moment.

"That's better. Now cast your eyes on this," Ted said, placing a spiral-bound booklet on the table. The burgundy cover bore an impressive seal and a heading announcing The 45th Annual Meeting Of The International Society Of Classical Archeologists. Ted flipped hurriedly through the book. "We're skipping the cocktail party and dinner tonight. Borrring. The morning talks are equally dispensable, but look at this." He pointed to the following afternoon's schedule. *Keynote: Report of Excavations in Thera, Dr. Theodore Gustafson, 5:00 p.m.*

"Wow. I'm impressed," she said genuinely. "You're a headliner."

"Wait until you catch my act," he replied with a grin.

"I already have."

"My *academic* act." He seized her hands in excitement. "I'm going to knock them dead, Julia. Atlantis exists. The Temple of Poseidon is down there. I know it. I've got the proof. It's like finding the goddamn Holy Grail. I'm so glad you'll be here to see it."

"Me, too," she said. "It'll be exciting."

"It'll get a lot of attention," he said. "I'm sure of it. Tomorrow night we'll really have something to celebrate."

"Tomorrow night I'll be back in L.A.," she reminded him gently. "I'll stay for your presentation and then head directly to the airport."

"Let's not talk about it now."

"You know I can't stay any longer. I shouldn't be here at all."

"But you are here. And you look so beautiful and I am incredibly lucky to be with you."

He reached across the table, framed her face with his fingers and gently kissed first one eyelid, then the other. Her eyes were still dreamily closed when she felt a heavy hand press upon her shoulder. Startled, she looked up into a ruddy face that looked astonishingly like a clean-shaven, older version of Ted. The large, red-haired man stood like a bridge, one hand on her shoulder, the other on Ted's, smiling broadly. "Well, if it isn't brother Theodore, here in town and hasn't even looked us up."

"I just got in today—" Ted began.

"Didn't tell us you were coming, either. Isn't that downright unfraternal, Cass?"

Cass, a towering blonde with frizzy curls, sheathed in a red satin minidress, smiled in agreement.

"You must be Ann," the man said. "I'm Roger, Ted's big brother."

"This is Julia," Ted said evenly.

Julia nodded, grateful for Ted's quick intervention but wondered, with a pang of jealousy, if the relationship with Ann were not as casual as he had implied.

"Well, who can keep track," Roger said amiably. He grinned, revealing strong, tobacco-stained teeth. "No offense, miss." Then, turning his attention to Ted, he continued, "I knew you'd be here for the meeting, Teddy boy. Big mistake. They're going to burn your ass."

"What are you talking about?" Ted demanded.

"I hear the boys from Berkeley think your Atlantis paper is a crock of shit." He glanced at Julia. "Pardon my Greek."

"Stick around and find out, Roger." Ted downed the remainder of his drink.

"I aim to do just that," he said, pulling out a chair for Cass.

Ted rose to his feet. "Roger, this isn't a good time. We were just leaving."

"Nonsense." Roger drew his chair closer, signaling to

the waitress. "Everybody's got time for a drink, right?" He paused, smiling at Julia. "I don't know what brother Ted's told you about me, probably not too much. We've been out of touch." He then turned to Ted. "There have been some changes. I left *Time Magazine*, left Ellie and the kids, left twenty years of bed and board. Now I'm a science stringer at the *Chronicle*. I'm covering the conference. New bed and not so bored. By the way, I hear you went bust and Mathilda bailed you out."

"It's a loan," Ted said. "I'll pay it back."

Roger shook his head in amazement. "Oh, man, have you no shame, fueling your Atlantis pipe dreams by conning your own mother?"

"It's an investment, Roger."

"Yeah, right up there with junk bonds."

Julia was disquieted by Roger's unflattering comparison. Was it jocular or was it meant as a true criticism? Either way, it was unsettling. Cass broke the awkward silence by turning to Julia, asking, "So when's your birthday, honey?"

"My birthday?" Julia said, puzzled. "February 20th."

"I knew it! A Pisces. On the cusp," Cass crowed. "When it comes to horoscopes, I am intuition a-go-go. Even though I am honestly on the ward today. On the ward. First our Beulah does not show, so I have to play Donna Reed, you know, do the dust mop shuffle. Then my mother, who is queen of the hypochons, is hysterical about her mammogram. So I call her doctor, who tells me Mama is on acid, that au contraire, her tits are normal, just somewhat dense. Kind of like Mama," Cass chortled. "Then Dodger and I have a big fight, followed by the obligatory heavy-duty Elmer's Glue session." She took a deep swig of her Scotch. "Believe me, honey, today was no day at the beach."

"I'm sure it wasn't," Julia muttered. Her own words seemed particularly colorless but it was all the rejoinder she could think of.

"Don't she talk up a storm?" Roger said with admiration. Then he continued speaking to Ted, as if there had been no interruption. "Unless, of course, you've actually discovered something."

"You'll find that out tomorrow." Ted placed some bills on the table. "We've got to go. See you around."

The big man was on his feet, his hand on Ted's sleeve. "How about dinner?"

"We've got plans for tonight," Ted said.

"Tomorrow then," Roger said, his voice soft, imploring. "No hard feelings. Come on, Ted. For old times' sake."

Ted studied his brother's face for a moment, then shrugged. "Sure, why not?"

"Great, Teddy Bear," Roger said, clapping him heartily on the shoulder.

Julia waited until they were out of earshot. "Did you understand what that woman, Cass, was saying?"

"Roger could always pick them. The weirder the better."

"She seemed friendly enough, though," Julia said. "She's probably a lot of fun."

"Well, she's certainly colorful," Ted conceded.

As they waited for the doorman to whistle them down a cab, Julie slipped her hand in Ted's. "Why did he call you Teddy Bear? Because you carried one?"

"Because I looked like one, fat and furry," he answered. "It was my nemesis all through high school."

"I wish I knew you then."

"I had a raging case of acne."

"My skin was perfect then," she said. "It breaks out now."

"Delayed adolescence?" he teased.

She studied him from under her lashes. "It would explain a lot."

And there was a lot to explain, she thought. About both of them. She wondered about his relationship with Roger. It seemed edgy, but curiously affectionate. Sibling rivalry? Testosterone tussles? And what was the banter about their mother?

"Taxi, sir," the uniformed and chevroned doorman confirmed as he held out his white gloved hand discreetly for the proffered tip.

As they entered the cab, Ted turned to her. "When choosing a dinner spot, what counts most for you— food, service or atmosphere?"

"Atmosphere," she said. "Hands down."

"Beauty, luxury or authenticity?"

"All three, but if I must pick…authenticity."

"Forty-eighth Avenue and Sloat Boulevard," Ted told the driver, "near the Great Highway."

They sat close together and watched as San Francisco flowed past—the tall white office buildings; the Geary and Curran Theaters with their lighted marquees; the small transient hotels. The Arab grocery stores with their one-portion cans and inflated prices; the adult bookstores, the massage parlors, the gay bars. They drove down the wide stretch of Van Ness Avenue, lined with gleaming automobiles encased in plate glass showcases, past the garish murals of Tommy's Joynt, home of the buffalo steak, out through the small businesses and apartment houses of the Richmond district, the greenbelt of Golden Gate Park, then through the Sunset, the alphabetical avenues of Santiago, Taraval, Ulloa, Vicente, Wawona, then a right turn toward the ocean. When they could smell the salt spray, the cab stopped.

Julia opened her purse to pay the fare. "Not necessary," Ted demurred. But Julia insisted. When she was with Mark, he paid for everything. It was the accepted way they operated. All those forged rituals. He always drove. She always did the grocery shopping. He did the taxes. She purchased the presents. He took out the garbage. She picked up the dry cleaning.

Julia felt a mixed sensation—pride in breaking a familiar pattern, for she had always been supported by men, first by her father, then by Mark, but also a touch of unease, as if the earth had shifted and the footing was precarious.

They climbed out of the cab in front of a white tiled diner with a revolving roof sign of an oversized grinning dachshund in a chef's cap. "Best pastrami sandwich in town," Ted said. "With cheese or without?"

"Without," she said.

"One kosher pastrami, one tref," he ordered. "Two fries, two Cokes. To go."

"Tref?" she asked. "Where did you learn that?"

"I went to graduate school at Columbia. I also know 'schmatte,' a rag; 'chutzpah,' overweening ego; 'tsuris,' trouble; 'mensch' an admirable person; 'schmuck'…the opposite. I can curse in eight languages, make love in six and excavate in four."

"The numbers are related to the significance of the task, I assume."

"The frequency," he amended.

They waited, admiring the precision of the short-order cook as he sliced and heated the spicy, delicious-smelling meat, piled it on sesame buns and handed her a juicy warm package that was already beginning to stain its wrapping.

"We're going to have a picnic at the beach, right?" she said.

"Too prosaic," he answered. "I'm thinking African safari." He took her free hand and led her in a traffic-dodging dash across the street to the stone pillars and steel gates of the San Francisco Zoological Society.

Julia read the sign upon the padlocked gates: Open Every Day 9:00 a.m. To 5:00 p.m. She checked her watch; it was seven-fifteen. "It's been closed for hours," she said.

"How inconvenient. Five's much too early for dinner," Ted replied, eyeing the gates. He stepped backward into the street, then, running forward, gathering speed, hooked one foot on a protruding stone, then the other, and catapulted onto the top. He sat astride the rock wall and waved in triumph.

"That's great, Tarzan," she called, "but Jane doesn't do her own stunt work."

"Piece of cake," he assured her. "Now step back to the curb, run as fast as you can, and I'll grab you."

Julia looked over her shoulder; a man and his poodle were watching with interest, as were some people in a passing bus. She had a sudden vision of a policeman and a jail cell. Dismissing the vision, she took a deep breath and sprinted for the wall. A running leap, a clawing scramble, Ted's arms beneath her shoulders and she was teetering beside him astride the wall, sheltered by the trees, closer to the sky. Triumphant, Ted sprang to the grass on the other side, and she followed, cushioned by his arms. It was then that she remembered the dinner bag outside the gate, where she had jettisoned it in preparation for the leap.

"Sorry," she said. "Should we go back and get it?"

He shook his head; there was adventure in access, not in retrieval. "We'll forage in the forest. Live on nuts and berries."

A few yards down the path he whooped with pleasure as he spied a candy machine. "Manna from heaven," he cried as he emptied his pockets of quarters and pulled the levers. He divided the spoils—two chocolate bars apiece. Julia let the first bite of chocolate dissolve fully in her mouth, melt into a rich dark puddle, coat her tongue then slide down her throat like a sweet glacier. She licked the last of it from her teeth and grinned. "Chocolate is my favorite indulgence."

"And, you, madam, are mine," he said as he gently kissed her mouth. She tasted him, chocolate on chocolate. He laughed deep in his throat. "At how many points can we join?"

"Connect the dots and find out," she said, holding him close. "That's how I feel," she whispered, "that you are a lovely, thick felt-tip pen that has connected my dots in one long flowing line. Inside and out."

They were at a playground now, a jumble of abandoned equipment. Julia strode across the grass to sit in one of the swings, the sand in her shoes recalling all those former playground times, first as an awkward child, then as a reluctant mother. Ted seized the chains of an adjacent swing and leaped astride its canvas seat, his head almost grazing the supporting frame. She watched as he stood tall and pumped vigorously, causing the swing to rise in widening arcs, higher and higher. It was something she had always wanted to do, but had been stopped by fear of falling. Now she wanted to try it. She jumped down, kicked off her high-heeled sandals, pulled back the canvas seat and, as it swung forward, jumped on, moving with its natural momentum. Then, pumping her knees and elbows, she sent the swing into a wide soaring arc. "Hey," she called, "look at me. I never could do this before."

"Swing?" he asked.

"Swing standing up," she replied.

He jumped off his own swing onto the sand, broke a small branch from an overhanging tree and, holding it like a microphone, intoned, "And now, sports fans, we will hear from the athlete herself, how she accomplished this astonishing feat, the first of her career. Julia, oh, Julia, may we have a word with you for our cameras? Will you share with us, at this moment of personal triumph, the secret of your success?"

Julia took the proffered branch, raised it to her lips with a weary smile. "I can say it in four words—courage, discipline, natural rhythm."

"Thank you, Julia," he said, snatching back the stick. "I'm sure you'll want to be heading off to the showers. Let that be an inspiration to you, all you little pigtailers out there, all you middle-aged housewives. Slip off your shackles and swing!"

"You ain't seen nothin' yet," she exclaimed, climbing the ladder of the slide and swooshing down its damp metal tongue, backward. Ted countered with hanging by his heels on the monkey bars while she peered at him from below. They then engaged in a mock power struggle on the seesaw, Ted stubbornly, leaden assed on the ground, keeping Julia suspended, feet dangling in the air. At her vociferous complaint, he engineered a quick reversal that landed her with a jarring thump.

"Ouch," she cried. "How about a nice equilibrium? Like a good relationship…cooperation and sensitivity, equal flow, balance."

"How about 'I can't go up without pushing you down'?" he teased.

They passed a miniature roller coaster, airplane and cable car sequestered and shuttered for the night, then on to the area that held the sleeping merry-go-round. They climbed the makeshift fence to admire the circle of horses, lions and tigers, pigs and dogs. There was a pink ostrich cart for the timid, a gray cat with an orange fish in its mouth, a green-and-white-striped zebra, and a silver unicorn, as aloof and magical as a tapestry on a castle wall. And off at the side stood the wooden arm holding the brass rings.

It took courage to lean way out from the galloping horse and reach for the ring. Once on a long-ago visit to San Francisco, Mark had caught a brass ring for Davey and presented it to the ride-attendant. "Just toss it back in the box," the man had said. "There are no free rides anymore."

Prophetic, Julia thought, as she watched Ted climb aboard the carousel. But maybe there never were.

The carousel hadn't changed much, still gilded and mirrored and painted with rosy cherubs. She remembered Davey, then a sturdy four-year- old in striped coveralls, waving dutifully each time his revolving steed passed her shivering form on the bench. The song was always "When you are in love it's the loveliest night of the year." Julia began humming the melody, and Ted, as he wandered among the animals, bobbed and weaved to its rhythm. The man who used to run the merry-go-round had been tall and pale, unshaven, she remembered. Silent, almost furtive. But he had carefully buckled the children in and retrieved their dropped tickets with unfailing patience.

"Hey, Ted," she said, boarding the carousel and scrutinizing him across the muzzle of the unicorn. "What about kids?"

He looked about. "Don't see any. They're all home torturing their pets."

"Do you want some?"

"Not today."

"Ever?"

"Ever is way beyond my time frame." His fingers traced the spirals of the unicorn's horn. "Right now, I've got enough taking care of me. I used every penny and then some to finance this past year at Thera. Now I've got to get those findings recognized, and raise the money for a major excavation. But, damn it, Julia," he said, eyes blazing, "I've found it. Plato's Atlantis. Just wait until tomorrow. Wait until it hits the press. They can take their goddamn tenure and shove it up their constipated asses."

"What tenure?" she asked.

He grinned, twirling the reins of his stallion like a

lasso. "Once I was a fair-haired boy at Yale, assistant professor of classical anthropology, specialist in Greek archeology. But it was publish or perish. You know that joke about Jesus…granted, he was a great teacher, but he didn't publish much."

"Is that why they let you go?"

"That, a few missed lectures, some freewheeling conjectures at a Journal Club instead of a report on nine thousand ceramic fragments…and I was out on my ear. Ah, hell, the only reason I wanted Yale was for the funding. But once my findings are validated, I'll get all the private backers I need."

As she climbed astride the unicorn the better to listen, she recalled the legend. The only way to snare a unicorn was to place a virgin in an open field, then the elusive beast would venture forth and willingly lay its head in her lap. How could the unicorn tell? she wondered.

"What do you expect to find?" she asked.

"Everything. A whole city preserved under a thousand feet of ash, like Pompeii. Shops and villas and thoroughfares, forums and baths and storehouses. But all of it underwater. And in the center, the gem, the sine qua non…"

"The Temple of Poseidon," she said, stroking the unicorn's roped and tasseled mane.

"Listen, this is Plato," he said, and recited the description as in a remembered dream. "'The Temple of Poseidon has something of the barbaric in its appearance. All the exterior of the temple they coated with silver, save only the pinnacles, and these they coated with gold. As to the interior, they made the roof all of ivory, variegated with gold and silver and orichalcum—'"

"What's orichalcum?" she asked.

"A kind of brass."

"Like the ring on the merry-go-round," she mused. "No free ride."

"What?" he asked.

"Nothing. Go on. I'm listening."

"'And they placed therein golden statues, one being that of the god standing on a chariot and driving six winged steeds,'" he continued. "'And round about him a hundred Nereids on dolphins and outside round about the temple, there stood images in gold of all the princes and their wives, as many as were descended from the ten kings.'"

She brushed the hair back from Ted's forehead, revealing even more of the dazzle of his eyes. He reminded her of Davey back from the circus, ablaze with excitement from the spectacle of the tumbling, flying bodies, the silks and satins, the drumrolls.

"How did Atlantis sink?" she asked.

"A volcanic eruption destroyed all of Thera and most of Crete. The explosion was felt throughout the Mediterranean, almost throughout the entire civilized world. We have records from more recent volcanic eruptions like Krakatoa. In 1883, when Krakatoa exploded, the sky went dark, one-hundred-foot tidal waves rolled as far as the coast of Japan and volcanic ash colored the world's sunsets for years. The explosive power was equivalent to four hundred and fifty hydrogen bombs. And after measuring the calderas, we estimate that Thera was five times the size of Krakatoa."

Julia shivered as she imagined that flood of fiery lava, the waves like mountains, the earth splitting, the darkness, the buildings tumbling, ships flung ashore, the screams, the chaos.

"That volcano eruption," Ted concluded, "was the most destructive natural event in the written history of man."

"Is that why you like it?" she asked.

"Could be," he said. "I do like action." He tugged at her hand. "Enough shop talk. Let's pay homage to the beasts, then get some dinner."

They followed a path that led to a deep stone pit, a leafless tree, and in the center a lugubrious gorilla, poking at his truck-tire swing. Ted read the identifying sign: "'Moustapha is a gorilla, gorilla, gorilla, native to the jungles of—'"

He was interrupted by a loud throat clearing, then another, even louder.

They turned to confront a burly uniformed man menacingly jangling a heavy ring of keys. "You people aren't supposed to be in here. Zoo's closed."

Julia moved closer to Ted. So here it was, the reprimand she had been expecting, the consequence waiting to pounce. Ted smiled disarmingly. "Sorry about that, sir. You see, the little lady and I just got married. I promised I'd take her someplace special like Africa, but this is as far as we got."

"It's after hours," the man chided.

Ted shrugged. "I know, but it's our honeymoon. We wanted to be alone."

"You've got to leave right now," the man said, "or I'll have to call the police." Then with a shrug, he gestured to the left. "Take the North Gate out. It goes past the big game."

"Thank you, sir. The missus and I really appreciate it," Ted said. Putting his arm about Julia's shoulders, he leaned forward to whisper, "Like the fat lady in the circus said, 'If you can't hide it, decorate it.'"

"You are shameless," she said as they walked away. Yet she couldn't help grinning. It was audacious and fun and hadn't hurt anyone. She felt like a kid again. Playful, risk taking. The world was new and exciting again. The unexpected was waiting around the next corner. They passed the giraffes, the elephants, the rhinos and hippos. The lions and tigers. Their own private safari.

As they approached the exit gate, Ted stopped at Monkey Mountain, a towering structure swarming with clambering rhesus monkeys, babies clinging to their mothers' backs, young males squabbling, white furred grandmothers washing their dinner in a trickling water-fall.

"We'll take our vows here," he said, "with all our rel-atives present."

"What vows?" she asked.

"You don't want to make a liar out of me." He reached down, plucked a long blade of grass, tied it around her thumb. "Your opposable digit," he pronounced, "sepa-rates us from the rest of the beasts." He kissed her fore-head, her lips, the cleft between her breasts. "I savor thee for thy playful mind, thy sweet mouth, thy loving heart. Will you be mine? Tonight?"

Her breath caught in her throat. It was playful, make-believe, but it was a ritual and it had meaning. She swal-lowed hard. "I will," she said. Then, plucking a daisy, she placed it behind his ear. "I relish thee for thy wicked smile, thy flame-gold hair, thy magical search. Will you be mine? Tonight?"

"Absolutely," he said. Wearing their adornments, they left the zoo and successfully hailed a cab.

Ted asked the driver to take them to a Greek taverna. "In honor of our missed moments in Athens," he said as they entered the Taverna Plaka on the edge of North Beach. The mustachioed owner led them to a small table on the edge of the dance floor where the orchestra, with its mournful bouzouki, played the swooping strains of a Greek folk song. They watched as the patrons linked arms and circled the floor, heels pounding the beat.

The food they ordered came on enormous platters—mounds of shiny green dolmas, crisp souvlaki, steaming rice and eggplant, salad garnished with plump tomatoes, feta and black olives, and round sheets of pita bread. They washed it all down with a bottle of mouth-puckering retsina wine, then thick black coffee and honey-drenched baklava. They were both hungry and ate with gusto and few words.

At the last sip of coffee, Ted rose and drew her to the dance floor. Julia's feet easily followed the recurring pattern of the simple, familiar melody, her body bending and weaving, carried by the strong current of the moving dancers. The circle was as buoyant and effortless as the sea. They danced through several numbers, stopping only when the musicians took a break.

When they returned to the table, Julia was quiet, lost in her thoughts. Ted traced her chin with his forefinger. "Hey," he said softly, "where did you go?"

"Back in time," she said, looking up to gauge his interest.

His gaze was focused and steady. "I want to hear anything you want to tell me."

She brushed at the bits of bread crumbs strewn upon the table as she summoned her words. "The first time I went Greek dancing was a few months after Wendy was born. I was very depressed, crying all the time, almost suicidal. I was going to a shrink, taking meds, but I still couldn't eat, couldn't sleep, couldn't even make a phone call. A friend, a Gestalt therapist, John Emory, suggested it. He and his wife led couples' marriage encounter groups and Greek dance. They've since split up," she added ruefully. "Guess it doesn't always work. At any rate, I didn't want to go that night. I was afraid. The noise in my head was so loud I couldn't speak, couldn't hear. Mark insisted, so we went. I remember John asking me how I felt, and the disparity between the truth and what was socially acceptable was so great that I froze. Mark had to answer for me.

"Then the music started and John grabbed my hand, wouldn't listen to my protests. He placed me between himself and another strong dancer, and together they led me through the steps. I didn't have to initiate anything, plan anything, just surrender to the music and be carried along. We must have danced for hours. I was bathed in sweat, panting, sore, but I was so high. It was as if a veil had been lifted, as if the ashes had been blown away. My life had been restored to me. Everything I needed was already there, perfect and shining—all I had to do was recognize it. Things were so clear. I understood what mattered. And I knew I would be all right." She paused, covered Ted's hand with hers. "It doesn't last forever, that clarity. But once you experience it, you remember it. Just as years from now, I'll remember tonight."

In answer, he kissed her fingers. "This one's for you," he whispered, then leaped to his feet to join the line of dancers. It was an all-male labyrinth dance from Crete, an intricate series of jumps and stamps and spiraling, celebrating the ancient springtime ceremony in which young acrobats seized the horns of a bull and jumped over its broad back. Ted took his turn as dance leader, leaping onto a tabletop, twirling and slapping his heels. He received a round of enthusiastic applause for his efforts and returned to the table breathless and jubilant, his shirt transparent with sweat.

He smelled musty and sweet. Julia leaned forward, kissed him on the temple, then playfully darted out her tongue, lizardlike, and speared a drop of moisture. He tasted like dried apricots. Mark's sweat tasted of garlic.

Even though he rarely ate the spice the acrid smell lurked in his armpits, beneath his tongue. When Mark would bend to kiss her, she would often offer her cheek rather than her lips. It had been years since she had kissed him openmouthed. She would acquiesce to sex; it was less intimate than a long, passionate kiss. She could tell him to freshen his breath. And yet she never had. It had become easier to maintain a distance.

When they left the taverna, the night was balmy. She didn't even need her coat. She and Ted walked, arms around each other's waist, into the bright lights and flashing neon of Broadway…Nude Co-ed Strip Contests, Naked Wrestling, Sex-a-rama, XXX-hibition Room. Ted surveyed the frenzy around them, the weaving cars, the pushing crowds, the hustling barkers, the blaring discos. "I lived in Thera for three years, working with our Greek crew," he mused. "We spent the mornings in the dig, dove in the wrecks all afternoon. Spent the evening in a taverna drinking ouzo and dancing. Slept it off in hammocks under the stars. We woke to the smell of warm bread and fresh goat cheese, purple figs and coffee thick enough to paint a house with. Those people spent each day in the shadow of a volcano, but they knew how to live."

"Californians live in the shadow of an earthquake. Sooner or later everything disappears," she said.

"And what will destroy us?" he asked.

"Time," she stated, drawing closer to his side. "And it's running out."

"Not yet. We've got our honeymoon trip."

"On a cable car?" she joked.

"On a chartered yacht."

He hailed a cab to Pier 39. They boarded the White Harbor Cruise Ship just as the departure whistle was blowing and the gangplank lifting. They eschewed the cabin and chose the outside deck. Leaning on the railing, they watched the wine-dark Pacific roll by, gazed at the necklaces of the two bridges, the stretch of Angel Island, the forbidding hulk of Alcatraz. They huddled together against the damp wind, sipped muddy coffee from foam cups, and watched an old man in a wrinkled overcoat feed bread crusts to the swooping gulls. The man waited patiently until the birds taxied in to spear them from his fingers.

"I hate seagulls," Julia said, frowning. "Ugly rapacious birds."

"Scratching out a living like the rest of us," Ted said.

"I don't like their mouths. They're like scissors. Or the desperate way they fight among themselves for any scrap of food."

"They're hungry," he said.

"They're always hungry and all they ever do is eat.

They eat anything...even garbage. Their only saving grace is they can fly."

He pressed his cheek against hers, his stubble grazing her skin, "Is that what you'd like to do? Fly?"

"Maybe."

"With me?" he asked.

She stepped behind him, hugging him for warmth. "I've got a job I like, two great kids, a comfortable house, a working marriage."

"The perfect life, the American dream. So what's missing?"

"Passion. Play. All that male-female stuff."

"You must have had that at the beginning. Everyone has that at first."

She shook her head. "Not me. I didn't know what it was. I was a poor girl from the Bronx with a B.A. in English lit. That and a quarter, as my father was fond of saying, would get me a ride on the subway. Mark was a promising young doctor. He was my chance for a house in the suburbs, a station wagon, two and a half kids. An identity. All at age twenty. And I liked Mark, he was big and bright and self-assured. He was also the first boy who ever took me to dinner and the theater on the same night.

"My engagement ring was a one-and-one-half-carat emerald cut diamond in a platinum setting. I wore it to school the week of my college graduation, and it caused a lot more excitement than my Phi Beta Kappa key. We became engaged at a nightclub in Brooklyn. Mark dropped the ring in my champagne glass and I almost swallowed it. That night, in celebration, we tried to make love, but I was so tight, we couldn't. So we promised to wait until we were married. That was fine with me."

"And did you wait until after the wedding?" he asked.

"Our wedding night was at the Plaza Hotel on Fifth Avenue. We had the bridal suite overlooking Central Park. Everything was decorated in red—red velvet upholstery, red satin sheets, red flocked walls, red plush carpet. I undressed while Mark was in the bathroom. I remember shedding my white lace bridal gown, white shantung shoes, white eight-foot tulle veil, floor-length white horsehair crinoline, white merry widow, white stockings, white silk underpants, and piling them up like a mound of whipped cream on a sea of cherry Jell-O. I put on my white trousseau negligee. Mark came out, wearing his white honeymoon pajamas. We turned out the lights, kissed, touched each other briefly. It was more like taking inventory, we were both so shy. Mark pulled out a tube of Vaseline jelly, greased us both, entered, stroked valiantly ten times, then collapsed on my breast saying, 'I love you. How was it?'"

"Well, how was it?" Ted asked.

"Sort of like the Emperor's New Clothes," she said, then suddenly felt disloyal. "I shouldn't be talking about this."

"Nonsense. Everyone's first sexual experience is more like Manischewitz than Montrachet," he said.

"Was yours?" she asked.

"Absolutely. And I'm still developing my palate," he said with a grin. "That's one of the best things about California. Great varietals. So how did a New York girl wind up here?"

"That was Mark's doing. I never would have had the courage to uproot. And it was a very good move." She felt grateful for the genuine loyalty.

They disembarked from the ferry and caught the last cable car to their hotel. It was crowded and they rode on the outside, clinging to each other for balance, laughing as the brakeman rang the warning bells, clearing the steaming tracks.

They piled off at the foot of the hill and climbed the few steps to the hotel. They were silent in the elevator approaching their floor. What now? Julia thought. The elevator ground to a halt. The doors opened. They walked down the corridor toward their respective rooms. Julia fished in her purse for her room card. She found it and slipped it in the slot. They both heard the accepting click, saw the light flash. Neither one of them moved.

"Green light," Ted said softly. "You're free to go."

She turned toward him, willing him to say something, do something, to take charge. But he was being true to his word. No strings. And yet there were strings; she felt them. Invisible connections that had grown between them, powerful threads of desire, of truth telling, of mutual discovery. It had been less than a day since they'd met. But was it not Rumi, the Sufi poet, who said that lovers don't find each other, they are in each other all along?

"Do you want to come in?" she whispered.

"Are you sure?"

She nodded, not trusting her voice.

He followed her in and shut the door. He drew her close. She was aware of his height and his wiry muscularity. She could feel his arousal. Her own body was trembling.

"You're cold," he said. And then to her surprise, added, "I'll draw us a bath." He entered the bathroom, then returned with a terry-cloth robe. "Put this on," he said. "And give me five minutes."

Julia slipped off her clothes, carefully folding the Greek outfit. It had done its job, made her feel desirable, sensual. She stood naked before the mirror, quickly appraising her body. Except for the light stretch marks along her belly and breasts she looked much as she had years ago, just a bit softer, rounder. She wondered how Ted would see her. He was the only man to have seen her naked other than Mark. Her heart began to beat faster, her hands became clammy, her throat dry. Familiar signs of fear and misgiving. She shouldn't be doing this. It was wrong. She had taken a vow to be faithful and had honored that vow for twenty years. Now she was about to break that promise. Once it was done it could not be undone. Infidelity. Deception. Betrayal. The possible consequences of that action loomed ahead. It could hurt Mark, her family, herself.

She slipped on the robe, tying the belt tightly. She couldn't go through with it. She would tell Ted. He would understand.

She knocked on the door of the bathroom. "Come in," he called. She entered to see him sitting at one end of the tub, buried in foamy bubbles up to his armpits, back propped up against the tiled wall. "Your bath is ready, madam," he said. "And so is your bath toy."

He looked like a kid, rosy and grinning, so pleased with himself that she laughed out loud. Somehow it all felt innocent, playful, almost wholesome. She shed her robe and climbed gingerly into the other side of the tub. It was just big enough for two. He reached for a washcloth, soaped it, then, resting her leg upon his knee, began to massage the sole of her foot. It felt wonderful. She could feel the tension melting away. Slowly he moved up her leg, paying careful attention to her toes, her ankle, gently kneading the muscles of her calf and thigh, stopping decorously at the curve of her hip and moving instead to the sole of the other foot. She closed her eyes and gave in to the sensation. Such pleasure. He meticulously, assiduously massaged her hands and arms, her shoulders and back. It seemed to last forever.

"Time to get out," he finally murmured. And she stood obediently as he wrapped her in the terry-cloth robe. She felt so loved, so well cared for. Brand-new.

She followed him into the bedroom as he removed the quilted spread on the large double bed and drew back the covers. She tossed away the damp robe and climbed in, luxuriating in the silken feel of the sheets against her skin. Bliss. She was floating in sensation. She felt his eyes upon her and reached for the blanket to hide her nakedness.

"No, don't," he said.

"At least dim the lights," she said.

"I want to see you. You're so beautiful."

His praise, the light in his eyes as he looked at her, melted her last restraint. What her mind had forbidden, her body longed for. Moved toward. It was almost as if the mock marriage ceremony at the zoo, the wedding feast at the taverna, the honeymoon cruise on the Bay had been real, had somehow sanctified this union. She lifted the other side of the blanket, inviting him in.

He lay beside her, inches away, gazing into her eyes. "Julia," he murmured over and over. "My wonderful love." When she could bear it no longer, she moved toward him, and they met in the center with an audible sigh, the same "aah" that follows the first sip of water after an all-day thirst. They lay that way for long minutes without moving, just holding each other, feeling the length and breadth of each other, the warmth of skin, the crevices and hollows, enfolding what before had only been imagined. Then they explored each other slowly, leisurely, with sensitive fingertips, as if they were reading poetry in braille.

"I love your breasts," he said, cradling them, kissing her nipples. "They're eloquent." He drew his hand along the high rim of her pelvis. "And these long slippery bones."

She traced the muscles of his arms, the curve of his chest, slid her hand lower to cup the rising stiffness. "There's a nice slippery bone, too," she teased.

And with her mouth still open in laughter, he bent and covered it with his own. That kiss was Noah's rainbow, Shakespeare's sonnet, Bach's cantata. Ted's mouth tasted of ginger. And it came to her with a rush of recognition…so that's what it's like, to kiss a mouth you long to kiss.

"So what kind of wine am I?" she asked.

"You," he said, running his tongue around the rim of her ear, "are a vintage claret, fragrant, flinty, full-bodied but a bit immature. You need to be laid in a dark cellar for five years. And," he added, his strong hands circling her hips, "rotated frequently."

They made love like guests at a Cordon Bleu banquet, sampling and savoring the myriad scents and textures and juices on offer. Coming back for seconds. Trying new combinations. Then, after the entwined caresses, as the excitement built, he climbed astride. He rode her for long moments, alternating gentle circles with deep thrusts, plunging and rocking, filling her, cleaving her to him, and she rose and came close, closer, but fell away. She could not peak, not yet. They were too new. Now the joy of being with him, of merging with him, of drinking in his breath and scent, were enough.

"Go ahead," she whispered at last, "I can't." And he went on without her, climaxing in a long, deep groan of pleasure. He buried his face in her hair, sighing with contentment as they lay curled together, sticky as raisin snails.

"You get an A plus for that, sweetie," he murmured.

"I'd give me a B minus," she said. "Well motivated but gets nervous at finals."

She ran her fingers over his smoothly muscled chest, an expanse of deeply tanned skin with an occasional tuft of fiery red hair, so different from the gray-black curls that sprouted like fur over Mark's body. Ted was broader than Mark, but half a foot shorter, exactly her height in heels. It was a whole different sense to walk with, to make love to a man she could see eye-to-eye with. And he was almost twenty years younger than Mark…under the chin, around the eyes, in the belly, in his cock. She had always thought thirty a perfect age for a man, thought so at twenty, thought so now. But what did Ted make of her? She was, after all, an older woman.

Letting her thoughts spill into words, she asked, "How do I compare with Ann? That's her name, isn't it, the woman you lived with?"

He scratched his beard. "Yeah, Ann."

Julia waited, then asked, "Is she better or worse than I am?"

"At what?"

"This."

"Different," he said.

"How?"

He yawned and stretched. "She studied belly dancing at the New School for three years. She can move muscles *Grey's Anatomy* hasn't charted yet."

"Is she pretty?"

He paused reflectively. "She's mistaken a lot for that English actress. The one in *Titanic*."

"Kate Winslet? So why me, when you were living with Helen of Troy?"

He raised her chin so their eyes met. "It's over; so why be miffed at someone who's thousands of miles away? Someone who was just the latest in a long string of attractive bodies?"

"How long a string?" she asked.

He reflected. "Well, I'm thirty-two. I've been bedding women since I was seventeen. Now, if you're going to start comparing yourself with each of them, you'll need a spreadsheet. Remember *Desiderata*," he said waggishly. "'Do not compare thyself with others, for there will always be someone younger and more zaftig.'"

"Next you'll be quoting *The Prophet*," she cried, punching him lightly in the shoulder.

"Only some good-night verse." He pulled her close to him, spoon fashion, his chin resting on her shoulder. "'Now I lay me down to sleep, I pray the Lord my soul to keep.'"

She waited for the rest.

Silence.

"There's more," she prompted.

"It's enough," he said, yawning fully, settling into sleep.

She lay awake, first finishing the prayer, then the dangling conversation. She waited for the familiar pangs of guilt and remorse to rise, but they were softened by the satiny aftermath of pleasure, the sweet bone-weariness. Tomorrow she would be home with Mark and the children, immersed once again in her usual life. But tonight, with a spreading sense of wonder, it was as if she was living in her body for the first time. And she wanted to remember it.

6

Julia awoke to see Ted leaning on an elbow, peering down at her. Through the veil of her lashes, she studied him.

"I see movement in the underbrush," he said.

"It is your mind playing tricks, *kemo sabe*," she mumbled.

He bent forward, aligned his mouth precisely with hers. They breathed together.

"We both taste stale," she said.

"Perfect sync."

She smiled, raked her fingers through the wiry thickness of his beard. "You know, before I got married that used to worry me the most. What would you do about the smells…bad breath, B.O., bathroom smells? How would you disguise them, and if you couldn't, would it disgust your partner?"

"And?" he asked.

"You do and it does, sometimes. But you go on anyway. So many little habits that drive you insane," she mused. "Like every time it rains Mark looks out the window and says, 'Lovely weather for ducks,' or when you ask him to pay back something he says, 'I'd rather owe it to you than do you out of it.' Or when he eats, he takes enormous mouthfuls that stuff his cheeks, and chews forever with loud wet smacks." She shook her head guiltily. "I guess everyone's irritating, though, when you're around them long enough. My father used to say, 'I didn't decogonize you' for recognize. He thought it was funny. And whenever he was certain of something he'd declare, 'No bout adoubt it.' My mother had this crazy habit of sticking her finger in her ear and rotating it madly. When I was a kid I thought I'd develop it at puberty like breasts and pubic hair."

Ted stretched and yawned widely. She counted three gold crowns and a shard of spinach from last night's moussaka. He caught her gaze. "Think I have any bad habits?"

"Other than that?" she asked.

"Other than what?"

She mirrored his yawn.

"What's wrong with yawning? It's a natural act. I needed the oxygen."

"You could cover your mouth."

"What for?"

"Hygiene. Esthetics. Manners."

"Manners," he scoffed. "They went out with spats. All that stuff—stifling yawns, excusing burps, opening doors…life's too short."

"You confuse change and progress."

"Progress is anything that makes you more yourself." Then, grinning at his own fervor, he ruffled her hair and loped to the window. "Round one," he said. "Return to your respective corners." As he pulled open the draperies, the morning sun illuminated his long muscled body and burnished his red-gold curls. He scratched at his chest and groin, stretched luxuriously. "Man, could I use some coffee."

Julia appraised the tight curve of his buttocks, so different from Mark's pear shape. "But it does have its uses," Mark had often said cheerily, patting his broad rear. "You can't drive a nail with a tack hammer."

She slipped out of bed and stood behind Ted, her hands caressing his hips with soft feathery strokes. Without turning, he slid his hands over hers. "I'll give you an hour to stop that." She slipped her hand between his legs, squeezed gently. He walked backward, not breaking contact, until they tumbled back into bed. Her fingers moved along his penis like a blind potter, like a giddy pastry chef, until he moaned with pleasure. "Hey, lady, you've got talented hands. Where did you learn all that?"

"Masters and Johnson, Book Two," she said. Then sliding her fingers up his stiff throbbing cock, she ringed the head and squeezed firmly.

They both watched as his organ shrank, softened and drooped.

"Oh, no," he said sadly, "I think you broke it."

"Just pulled out the plug. That's the squeeze technique, devised to cure premature ejaculation. The woman stimulates the man's penis almost to the point of ejaculation, then applies pressure, detumescence follows.... Soon he learns the control himself, hence lasts longer."

"Was that a problem in your marriage?"

"Yes, although it was years until we realized it. We thought sex was supposed to be efficient, the faster the better. It wasn't so bad at the beginning. It was in between babies that it got messed up."

He nuzzled her breast. "How?"

"I couldn't conceive. We tried on our own for two years, then sought professional help. Things were never the same. It was like dissecting a canary to find out why it wouldn't sing. First we each had a battery of tests. Awful. Expensive. Embarrassing. I had air and dye injected into my ovaries and a D & C as a precautionary measure. Then they discovered Mark's sperm count was low, too much volume, too few sperm. Although it takes only one to fertilize, that sperm has to come surrounded by friends. So they put him on vitamin E, took him off jockey shorts and hot baths. We screwed in an exaggerated missionary position and only at my designated fertile times, and then we were expected to copulate nonstop like rabbits. Still no luck." She stopped. "You don't want to hear all this."

"I want to know everything about you that I can. This sounds important."

"It was," she said. "Then they spun down Mark's sperm, injected it into my vagina by syringe. It was quite a scene—he would masturbate into a bottle in the doctor's office and I'd pick it up an hour later, my OB playing pander. When even that didn't work, other donors were substituted for my monthly fix…medical students mostly, good stock, similar coloring, proven fertility. Nothing doing. After three years of fertility clinics, we agreed to adopt a baby. The end's predictable. One month after we heard of an available baby—a college student had gotten pregnant while wearing a diaphragm—I missed my period. That was Wendy. And she was worth it…every bit of it."

"What about the canary?" he asked.

Julia traced the line of his shoulder. "It returned to its

cage, but stopped singing. It seems the case was not so unusual."

They showered together, and after much dropping and retrieving of the slippery and elusive little bar of hotel soap, returned to bed. This time he lifted her legs onto his shoulders, and kissed and licked her until she was on the brink of orgasm. When he entered her, they moved their hips in synchronous rhythm; she came first, he a close second, in a seismic rumble.

After they caught their breath, Ted called room service and ordered a sumptuous breakfast. As they waited for it to be delivered, Julia asked, "Ready for a little exercise?"

Ted laughed. "Not so soon, babe. You've heard about the refractory period."

"Not that kind of exercise," she said. "Watch this." She climbed out of bed, stood in the clear space by the window and executed a series of flowing but strenuous dance postures.

He watched in admiration. "Very nice. What was that?"

"Tai chi chuan. I do it every morning."

"Tai chi chuan…is that from Column A or Column B?"

She smiled and wiped her forehead with the edge of the sheet. She lay back upon the pillow. "Tai chi is a form of moving meditation. It's a series of postures, one blending into another, invented by a Taoist monk one thousand years ago, said to be inspired by his witnessing the struggle between a snake and a crane. It helps to still the mind, restore balance and lubricate every joint." She folded her hands kimono style. "My teacher, Master Choy, says that the secret of life is to glide with the tide." She grinned. "So put that in your fortune cookie and eat it."

Ted laughed. "You're beautiful when you do it. Sensuous and spiritual."

"That was just the short form, thirty-seven postures. The long form has one hundred. And the names are wonderful." She sprang to her feet and executed a series of positions, naming each in turn. "Grasp Swallow's Tail. White Crane Spreads Its Wings. Embrace Tiger and Return to Mountain. Step Back and Repulse Monkey. Fair Lady Works the Shuttles. Snake Creeps down Tree. Step Forward to the Seven Stars. Step Back and Ride the Ox."

"How do you remember all those names?" he asked.

"Easy. We literary types love metaphor," she said.

He watched as she executed the difficult sweep of Lotus Kick and the long bend of Arch the Bow. She stretched luxuriously, rubbing her hands slowly over her body, massaging the accumulated chi over her skin like invisible lotion.

She smiled at him, "Shall I teach you?"

"No thanks, babe. No fixed patterns for me. No thirty-seven perfect postures. I move to my own music. Never the same way twice. That's why I love the Minoans. Of all the ancients, they believed in the moment. Catch the joy as it flies. Which reminds me. Here are my metaphors." He leaned over the side of the bed and rummaged in his briefcase, extracting a portfolio of color photographs. He held them up for her to see. Beautiful frescoes of young pigtailed boys boxing with one glove, of swallows courting, of a spotted jaguar leaping while his gazelle victim stood frozen in fear. A sylvan scene of young girls picking flowers. Julia moved closer to investigate the wasp-waisted Theran maidens in colorful tiered skirts and short-sleeved bodices that bared their breasts. "Look," she said, "they've painted their eyelids and fingernails blue, and this one has even rouged her nipples."

A discreet knock sounded at the door. "Room service."

"Just a moment," Julia called, and retreated to the bathroom as the waiter rolled in the trolley laden with domed platters. When she came out, the table near the window was set with plates of crisp bacon and fluffy scrambled eggs, fragrant coffee and flaky croissants atop linen heavy and white as parchment, with gleaming silver and a crystal bud vase holding one perfect yellow rose. She slid into the waiting chair. Ted looked up from the *Chronicle* and laughed with pleasure. She was wearing a long silk blouse fully unbuttoned to reveal her rouged breasts.

He leaned across the table and delivered a kiss to each nipple, then paused contemplatively. Puzzled, he kissed them again, running his tongue about them until they stiffened. "They taste different," he mused.

"A discerning palate. One's strawberry, one's peach."

"Now how did you manage that?"

"Fruit-flavored lipsticks."

"Delicious." He sampled them again, then, resuming his seat opposite her, studied her with approval. "You ought to dress that way all the time."

She grinned and slathered her croissant with two pats of butter.

They ate everything down to the last flakes of croissant speared from the tablecloth, read Doonesbury, and Dear Abby, and the daily horoscope aloud, shared the last pour of coffee still steaming hot from its silver pot.

Ted checked his watch. "It's barely ten. We've got the whole day free. What would you like to do?"

"Aren't you going to the conference?"

"To hear those other guys? Boring. How about a game of tennis instead?"

"That'd be fun," she said. "If you're sure you can get away."

"Baby, I can get away with anything. Suit up. I'm going to whip your ass."

"We'll see about that, big talker."

"Meet you in the lobby in twenty minutes," Ted said, and left for his room to change.

Julia stared at the phone. She was eager to talk to her children, to reassure herself that at least that part of her world was still in place. If she called home now, she reasoned, Mark should be making hospital rounds and she could avoid another confrontation. She dialed home. Davey answered on the first ring, his voice surprisingly deep.

"It's about time," he said. "You've been away forever. There's nothing to eat in the house."

"I missed you, too, sweetie. How's camp? How's Wendy?"

"Our team won the volleyball tournament. And Wendy passed her swimming test. The hamster's sick. His eye is all gooky." And Davey proceeded to give her a rundown of the household events.

As Julia listened, she could hear the shower turn on in the adjacent hotel room. She imagined Ted naked, stepping under the spray, remembered the weight of his body on hers, his mouth devouring hers. She could still feel him inside her. She gasped aloud.

"Are you okay, Mom?" Davey asked.

"Fine," she managed to answer.

But she wasn't. Her mind refused to accept the juxtaposition. It was like those books on parapsychology she had once read, on astral projection and out-of-body experiences. It was too much to accept. It shattered the givens of her known reality, and this time she wasn't curled up on the couch with an apple and a book. This time she was in the center of it, the prime mover.

"Wendy wants to talk," Davey said.

A moment's pause, then the soft whispery, "Hi, Mommy, when are you coming home?"

"Tonight, baby."

"What time?"

"After you're asleep."

"Daddy said before," Wendy protested.

"I bought you a surprise from Greece," she said with a guilty deflection. "I think you're going to like it. Okay?"

"Okay," the child said. "Do you want to talk to Daddy?"

With an involuntary shiver, Julia realized she had been lulled into thinking that she was safe. "Yes," she said, "sure."

"Julia?" Mark's tone was guarded. "What's up?"

"Nothing. Just called to say hello. And I might be a little later than planned."

"How late?"

"Maybe ten."

"Why?" he demanded.

"The talk I want to hear has been rescheduled to five."

"That must be some important talk," he said.

"It is," she said. "I'll tell you all about it when I get home."

"So what are you doing the rest of today?"

"Going to play tennis," she said, relieved to be telling the truth.

"Oh? With whom?"

"Someone…some people from the conference."

"That's convenient. I know how much you like to play."

"Right. Well, thanks."

"Bye," he said and hung up the phone.

She reviewed the conversation in her mind. Did Mark suspect? Did he mean anything by "That must be some important talk" or "That's convenient"? Or was she reading into his statements? Was his tone particularly cool, brusque? It was hard to tell. Some couples ended all their phone calls with "I love you." She and Mark never had. Why? she wondered. What was wrong with them? With their marriage?

Let it rest, she thought, let it remain hidden. But despite herself, she saw a sudden vision of Oedipus on a vast stone stage probing for the secret relentlessly until his sin lay naked and twisting before him and the stage ran red with blood, Jocasta's corpse and his own sightless orbs. The kingdom destroyed, the children homeless, all victim to the need to know. But that was catharsis. The essence of human tragedy. The need to seek the truth.

She hurriedly changed into her tennis gear, grabbed her racket and headed for the lobby. She found Ted in front of the notice board listing *Excavations at Thera— T. Gustafson*. It was listed among the other major presentations of the day: *The Palace of Pylos, The Olympic Stadium at Nemea, Shipwrecks of the Aegean.*

"Those other talks look kind of interesting," Julia remarked as they walked through the lobby and out the revolving door.

Ted shook his head, "Who cares about the competition?"

"Big mistake." They followed the voice to see Roger leaning against the outside wall, lighting a cigar.

"Just happened to be in the neighborhood?" Ted asked.

"Hardly. I've been waiting for you two to surface. I know it's a romance, but the flesh has its limits." He smiled and blew a wobbly smoke ring. "It's a mistake not to stick around for the earlier talks, Teddy boy. Arouses bad feelings. No one can have too many friends."

"They're hardly friends," Ted scoffed.

"Competitors, then, but they're here in droves, including Almighty Zeus himself direct from Thera."

"Valanopolis?" Ted's jaw tightened. "What's he doing here?"

"It seems the advance abstract of your paper has filled him with royal ire. He's here to refute it." Roger pulled a printed sheet from his pocket and read it out loud. "'American scientist illegally removes Minoan antiquity from excavation site. Artifact claimed to be the head of Poseidon a fraud. Atlantis speculations won't hold water.'"

"Where did you get that?" Ted asked.

"It's Valanopolis's statement to the conference, Teddy boy. He put it in every mailbox. You're going to have a fight on your hands."

"I'm ready for it."

"Are you, Ted? I think you're in deep water."

"But I'm a good swimmer, Rog. Remember, you're the one who taught me?"

The big man moved closer, banter over. "Let me help you, Ted. Let's talk about it, go over your paper. Your claims are extreme. Let's modify it. Look, why not just ask for the sonar testing to search for underwater canals? If you find them, that'll be discovery enough. This other stuff—the gold, the statues, the hundred Nereids riding dolphins—sounds like Marvel Comics."

Roger's tone had changed, Julia noted. The jesting was gone. He sounded genuinely concerned and what he said made sense. Why wasn't Ted listening?

"'If you don't believe in miracles you're no realist,'" Ted countered. "Ben Gurion said that, and he's right. Any idiot can excavate a ditch, patch pottery, reconstruct walls. Christ, man, I'm not interested in playing with LEGOs. This is the time for a leap of faith and I'm going to make it."

"Over Valanopolis's dead body," Roger retorted.

"It's just a power play with Val. He wants the money for the land excavations and I want it for the sea."

"He's got the clout," Roger warned.

"And I've got the proof," Ted said flatly.

Roger studied the set of his brother's shoulders and chin, then sighed. "I'll be there for the fireworks. And don't forget, you two are coming to our place afterward, no matter what."

"Thanks," Julia said, "but I won't be here."

"Why not?" Roger asked.

"Julia's got to go home to her husband," Ted said.

Roger's eyebrow lifted. "Another time then. You'll come, Ted?"

"Let's see how things go," he demurred.

"Come on, we haven't seen each other for three years. We *are* brothers." He held out his hand.

Reluctantly, Ted clasped it. "Okay, then, a victory celebration."

"He means well," Julia said as they walked away. "I think he's very fond of you."

"He and my mother have been trying to tame me forever and it hasn't worked." To illustrate, Ted grabbed hold of the nearest lamppost and, to the amusement of the passing crowd, hung horizontally upon it, his body stiff as a flag in the wind. Julia applauded his feat. She was with a wildman. She might as well make the most of it.

When he jumped back down, they crossed the expanse of Union Square, with its tiered fountain and majestic palms, and continued along Geary Boulevard, which was lined with Saturday morning street artists. They wove their way amid a juggler swallowing fire, a tuxedo-clad, white-faced mime who mirrored Ted's strutting walk and Julia's responsive laughter, two tap dancers, a trumpeter in a gorilla suit, and a Hare Krishna contingent with shaven heads and saffron robes stoned on bliss and bells. On past the couples holding hands, the tourists shivering in pastel cottons, the dogs eyeing fire hydrants, the whistles of doormen and traffic cops. They walked to the bus stop, where an exhaust-belching, red-and-white 38 Geary stopped for them. They rode it through the bustling Richmond, past myriad Asian shops and markets and restaurants, then caught the Muni 10 into Golden Gate Park.

At the stone lions of the De Young Museum, they disembarked. Julia led them on a quick foray through the wooden gates of the Japanese Tea Garden, donated by San Francisco's sister city, Osaka, to view the red-tiered pagoda, the towering stone Buddha, the shallow pool with its arched bridge and floating water lilies. She removed a coin from her change purse and threw it over her shoulder into the water.

"What did you wish for?" Ted asked.

"To beat you six-love," she replied.

"Never." He seized her hand and they raced down the path to the tennis courts, past tarnished statues of the city fathers, walls of rhododendron and a Shakespearean garden planted with every flower and herb mentioned by the Bard. Then, skirting bicyclists and toddlers and loping German shepherds, they ran past the glass hothouse of the arboretum, its flower plaque spelling out Welcome Archeologists in layers of succulents with an image of a pick and shovel below, outlined in golden chrysanthemums.

They jogged up the steep slope leading to the tennis clubhouse, Ted pulling her the last of the way. "You won by a nose," she gasped, "only because yours is longer."

He threw his arms around her neck and kissed her hard. "You are one gracious loser."

She laughed and licked her lips. "And you are one juicy kisser."

Hands entwined, they entered the clubhouse. A tall tanned couple stood, backs turned, ahead of them. They looked familiar, Julia thought. Something about the man's balding head, the woman's ropy-muscled calves. The woman turned to confirm it. "Julia, what a surprise," she cried. "What are you doing here?" She leaned forward, brushing a kiss on Julia's cheek, her eyes never leaving Ted. "Harry, look it's Julia Simon."

Harry Sokolov, a burly man with a beer belly lifting his mesh Lacoste shirt, smiled in greeting but sheepishly avoided Julia's eyes, confirming her suspicion that she and Ted had been observed.

"Roz and Harry Sokolov," Julia said, "this is Ted Gustafson." Hurriedly, she added, "Ted's an archeologist. We're both attending a conference at the Saint Francis. Ted's presenting a paper that's related to my subject area." She stopped abruptly. TMI, the kids called it. Too much information.

Roz tugged at a loose thread on her racket and looked about. "Sounds interesting. Is Mark here? We can all have lunch."

"No, he's at home," Julia stated.

"He works too hard," Roz said, "a slave to his practice. After that heart attack Harry's learned to take it easy, to live a little. We take a weekend away every few months now. We all should. Life's too short. Well, see you at the club, dear." A big smile for Ted. "Nice meeting you, young man. Enjoy your game."

Julia stared after their figures long after they were gone. Ted tossed her a tennis ball. She caught it reflexively. "Hey, babe," he said with a grin, "this *young man* is enjoying the game. Are you?"

"Oh, God. Roz Sokolov. She can't wait to spread the word. She's probably on her cell phone this minute."

"How well do you know them?" he asked.

"He's an orthopedist with an office in Mark's building, and they belong to our tennis club. We know a lot of the same people." She tightened her grip on her racket handle. "What rotten luck running into them. Her eyes just oozed malice."

"I thought it was envy."

"The thought is father to the deed. I wonder how much she saw."

"Something you want to hide?" he asked.

"If anything does come out, I'd just rather it came from me."

"Is it going to come from you?"

She shrugged, silent, troubled.

"Hey, guys. Can I help you?" the man behind the counter asked, his tone indicating that he had been asking the question for some time. The courts would change in ten minutes, he informed them, and they would be fourth on the waiting list. Since there were two dozen courts, the chances were good that they would get on. The man appraised Julia's outfit. White shorts, white T-shirt, white sneakers passed muster, but he cast a critical look at Ted's sweatshirt and jeans. "Only tennis shoes on the court," he admonished.

"Fair enough." Ted placed his foot upon the shelf outside the window, displaying his gray tattered sneakers, a circle of black sock showing through the ripped sole.

"Conspicuous nonconsumption," Julia chided as they sat in the sunlight watching tennis players arrive, pair off and move toward their courts. She watched as a quartet of young men, their long tanned limbs dusted with golden hair, warmed up with companionable jibes. They hit the ball with a clean sweep of motion from knees to hip, from shoulder to wrist, firm and straight as a bow releasing an arrow. They practiced their serves and volleys, and then the favorite shot of all young men, the overhead smash. She watched as they took quick darting steps backward to sight a lob, all attention on the spiraling fuzz of the ball, then a scissoring leap, a grunt and the ball was smashed away, sometimes on the court, sometimes over the fence, but always unreachable, un-returnable, decisive.

There were lovely girls, too, in crisp, dazzling white dresses that showed off their smooth tapered limbs, their elegant wrists and ankles. A diminutive Chinese maiden, her pigtails swaying to below her waist, pivoted with effortless ease to send the ball deep into her opponent's court time after time, patiently moving it from one side to the other until her opponent, growing increasingly shorter of breath and more erratic, missed.

A one-armed man bounced the ball over his head to begin his serve. A foursome of old men wore baggy white trousers, three almost skeletons, the fourth burdened with the weight the others had lost. No one ran; it was as if each had an invisible circle around him. If the ball fell within it, it was infallibly returned, if not, the point was conceded and a new volley begun. A classic example of knowing one's limits, Julia thought. Did she know hers? She used to, but they were changing. And it was both exhilarating and unnerving. She checked the clock. "Five more minutes."

"Five more hours," Ted corrected, "then it will all be part of history."

"Right," she said. He hadn't forgotten his presentation, not for a moment.

The loudspeaker bellowed the names of those souls

in limbo. She and Ted got the last available court, a good sign. Ted produced an open can of gray balls and put them into play. Julia hit the ball twice, then caught it. "These are dead," she said. "Let's get some new ones."

"Not necessary," he protested, "just hit them harder." She walked to the net, where she had left her purse. He came to meet her. They stood, separated by the white mesh barrier. As she fumbled for her wallet, he stood watching. "You do have a thing about the right equipment," he said.

"It's not a *thing*," she protested. "Dead balls spoil the game, that's all."

"They *change* the game," he amended. "*Spoil* is a value judgment."

"Okay, then, that's my value judgment."

She returned with a can of bright yellow, high bouncing Australian-made Dunlops and began the rally in earnest. In contrast to Julia's smooth, well-coached strokes, Ted's movements were awkward and unorthodox, sometimes combining the elements of a Ping-Pong chop, a baseball swing and a volleyball scoop. Yet somehow the ball kept coming back over the net. He was able to get to almost anything and in some manner return it, although the speed and angle of his shots were unpredictable. He seemed happy rallying, but Julia soon grew restless.

"Want to start a set?" she called.

"Sure," he said, spinning his racket. "Up or down?"

"Up," she said.

He read the handle. "Down. I'll serve. Which side?"

"This side's fine," she said. And as he took a stance in preparation to serve, she asked, "Taking some?"

He paused to reflect, then shook his head. "These go."

He threw the first ball up and sliced at it in a swift cutting motion. It hit the net. The next was three feet long. He retrieved the balls, but instead of serving into the ad court, prepared to serve again into the deuce.

"What are you doing?" she called.

"First one in."

"You said you were playing those."

"That's when I thought they'd go in," he said with a grin.

"You can't do that. You can't change the rules when you don't like the result."

"You sure are taking this game seriously."

"I just think you ought to stick to what you said, that's all. I don't care about the point," she declared.

"In that case, since I do, I'll take first in." He threw up the ball and hit a deep hard serve to her backhand, which grazed the tip of her racket and rolled out-of-bounds. "Fifteen-love," he called. She realized that she did care about the points as he went on to win game after game. There was no pattern to his play; he alternated dinks and winners in bewildering array. Her own rhythm and accuracy began to flag and with it her spirits, patience and goodwill. They played two sets and he won both handily.

On a crucial point in the third set, after she had hit two consecutive overheads, which he had somehow managed to shovel back, on his third lob, in a cathartic purge, she powdered the ball with every ounce of her strength. It landed six inches past the baseline. She let her racket slump, only to look up and see the ball come floating back over the net.

"Hey, what's going on?" she cried.

"Play it," he shouted.

Belatedly, she flung up her racket; it grazed the ball, sending it flying over the fence. "Why did you do that?" she demanded. "My ball was way out."

"Just a tad," he said. "I could reach it, so I played it."

"That's damned patronizing." She strode to the net and pulled on her sweater.

"To whom?" he asked.

"To me," she said, stuffing the balls into the can. "I don't need any favors. You did it several times, in fact—played 'out' balls. It threw my whole game off."

"That I wasn't predictable?"

"That you weren't playing by the rules."

"I often don't, Julia. It's more fun that way."

"Not for me." The weight of her words caused a surprising bodily reaction—a trembling of her lips, a heaviness in her chest, a growing closure in the throat.

"Hey," he said softly, stepping over the net and folding her into his arms, carefully, as if she might break. Holding her, meshing with her, waiting until her breathing stilled and her tears came, tears for breaking the rules. The wider rules, the rules that mattered. Pulling back, she worried about the spectacle they presented for the gallery, for the other players. Hopefully, the Sokolovs had departed. She was not used to public displays of emotion. And yet her outburst had been cathartic and had brought about the comfort of Ted's understanding. Perhaps the reticence of her marriage, the denial and burying of conflict, was not always the best strategy.

"Sorry," she said. "That was silly."

"Low blood sugar," Ted said. "We need a break. Lunchtime."

They left the courts and headed out to a nearby Richmond deli, where they assembled an impromptu San Francisco feast—a loaf of crusty sourdough bread, a wedge of Sonoma blue cheese, a plump pistachio-studded salami from North Beach, a bottle of sparkling Calistoga water and a fine Napa Valley cabernet. They strolled back to the park, found a grassy slope and laid out their feast. "Manna for the gods," Ted pronounced. He cut a wedge of bread with his pocketknife, piled it high with cheese and salami and handed it to her. She was touched by his thoughtfulness. Mark always served himself first. Then she chided herself for being unfair. This was courtship, not a long-term marriage.

"Thank you," she said.

He prepared a sandwich for himself and began to eat with gusto. He looked up to see her still holding hers, untouched.

"Aren't you hungry?" he asked.

She shook her head.

"Are you still upset about the bone doctor and his wife?"

"I'm still thinking about it."

"Why? It's over."

"It's just that things are starting to become difficult. Yesterday everything just flowed—the flight, the zoo, the taverna—but today...that phone call to Mark, seeing the Sokolovs, the tennis ...it's as if the grace period is over." She reached down and drew his hand to her cheek; the garlic and cheese smell was so redolent it made her smile. "I want it to be perfect until it disappears."

"Like the fabled Atlantis," he said, "destroyed in a single day and night."

"By a force of nature," she said.

"According to Plato, it was divine retribution. 'The ruling kings of Atlantis were once exemplary and supremely blessed, but in the course of time they fell away from their high standards and became greedy and domineering, whereupon Zeus, wishing to chastise them, called a council of the gods and spoke as follows....'"

Julie waited. "Go on," she urged.

"The *Critias* breaks off there. Plato never finished it. No one knows why."

"But why did the kings lose everything?" she asked.

"According to Plato, 'when the divine portion began to fade away and became diluted with the mortal admixture, human nature got the upper hand. They behaved in an unseemly manner and grew visibly debased. They were losing the fairest of their precious gifts, but to those who had no eye to see true happiness, they appeared glorious and blessed.'"

"The seeming and the being," she mused.

"And what is true happiness?"

She nodded; it was almost as if he could read her thoughts.

"It's a fleeting state of being," he said, handing her a plastic cup of wine. "The song got it right. Don't worry. Be happy." He unlaced her tennis shoes, slipping them off and cradling her bare feet in his palms.

She watched as he massaged the bottoms of her feet,

the spaces between her toes, kneading the ankles, the taut Achilles tendons.

"I remember your liking this." He grinned.

She felt herself dissolving into his hands. And she was swept with such a wave of feeling for him, a great warm rush, drenching her to her core, that she gasped and sputtered with it. "I think I'm falling in love with you," she said.

In answer, he bent and slowly, ceremoniously, kissed each of her toes.

She watched with the same flash of recognition that she had felt at the birth of her babies. Something extraordinary, something she had only previously imagined, was happening to her. Something timeless. Universal. So this was romantic love. What she had hoped for, dreamed of, longed for during a repressed girlhood where passion was to be feared and avoided, where lovemaking was restricted to chaste kisses and fumbling touches barricaded by clothing. She had remained a virgin, aided by tiny breasts and a body she was unsure of. It was easy to keep ardent hands off padded cotton and bony flesh. Then virtue rewarded, an early marriage, a sexual initiation.

Her first orgasms had occurred years later, after reading Masters and Johnson. Then while Davey napped, she had experimented with clitoral self-stroking and finger probings accompanied by a tattered copy of *Fanny Hill* for dialogue and the *Joy of Sex* for images. She pondered sharing her discoveries with Mark, but by then their relationship was fraught with tension, their lovemaking cold and mechanical. The haze and aura of her growing sensuality, of her solo explorations, led to flirtations at parties, speculations, fantasies culminating in the eventual selection of Michael. A choice that was, alas, not reciprocated. So the kernel of sexual energy, of life force, had hung suspended until she met Ted. Then, like a paper flower dropped into water, it opened, expanded, became full and fleshy and succulent. Yet she had spoken of "love" and Ted had said nothing in return, only a tender wordless gesture. She swirled her half-filled cup and watched the wine rainbow in the sunlight.

"Finished?" Ted asked. She nodded and he downed the remainder of her wine in a single long swallow, then ran his tongue appreciatively over his lips.

"You are a graphic person, my dear," she mused. "You lick your lips when something tastes good, rub your stomach when you're hungry, scratch your head when you're thinking. Strong body language."

He lifted his hand to cup her breast. "What does this say?"

She bent her head so that her hair curtained his fingers. "It says too public," she murmured.

"Ouch!" he cried.

She pulled back, startled.

"Not you, sweetie," he said, holding up a yellow plastic Frisbee that had just grazed the back of his head. "Struck down by a UFO." Ted laughed.

She twirled the object on her finger, studying the underside. "It's a flying saucer made in Taiwan."

"An Amazon breast shield," he said.

"Half of a giant yo-yo."

"A diaphragm for the bionic woman," he added.

"A pool of congealed butter."

"It's my Frisbee, mister, give it here." A skinny black kid, about thirteen, in a towering Afro and ripped cutoffs, thrust out his hand, inches from Ted's face. The kid tried a swift grab, his dirty fingers grazing Ted's beard. "Give it," he muttered.

"Not if you ask like that," Ted said.

"Listen, mothah, hand it over or…"

"Or what? You'll call a cop?"

The kid broke into a thin, grudging smile. "Yeah, right on."

"Sit down, friend." Ted patted a place beside him. "Have a bit of wine."

The boy squatted on his heels and stuck out his hand for the glass. Julia threw Ted an admonishing glance.

Ted lifted an eyebrow. "In La Belle France, wine is like

mother's milk and the young gentleman has already identified me as a mothah. I'm Ted," he said, pouring a tiny dollop in the boy's glass.

"Alfred," the boy muttered, and drank it down.

"A bit of sustenance?" Ted passed the boy a slice of bread topped with a wedge of blue cheese.

Alfred drew the offering to his nose, sniffed, grimaced, flung the cheese over his shoulder and stuffed the bread into his mouth. "Don't like no cheese. Smells like cat's vomit."

"Colorfully put," Ted said. "Some salami?"

The boy shook his head and held out his glass for a refill.

"I think you've had enough," Julia intervened.

"Don't worry, lady, I drink more than that for breakfast."

"What you do at home isn't my concern," she began. "But what you do here…" She stopped as she watched Ted put another small splash into the boy's glass, this time, to appease her, adding water.

Alfred grinned broadly, gave Ted a slow wink. "Thanks, my man, you all right for a spook."

"This spook's got game," Ted replied. "You ready?"

In answer, the boy placed his wineglass on the grass, ran several yards backward and flung the Frisbee skyward in a soaring arch, while Ted, galloping across the meadow, oblivious to potholes and boulders, leaped into the air for a fingertip catch. The meadow rang with their shouts and taunts as they chased the toy, darting and swooping and catching it behind their backs, making it curve first one way and then the other to land a few tantalizing inches from an outstretched hand.

"Alfred's the master!" Ted cried finally, falling breathless onto the grass.

"You run your ass off for an old dude," Alfred conceded between rasping breaths.

"High praise. Salud." Ted lifted his wineglass and clinked it against the boy's.

"Salud," Alfred said solemnly. He downed the last dregs of his watered wine, took his Frisbee and, offering a shoulder shrug in lieu of a wave, ambled off.

Ted winked at Julia. "Every great social occasion demands a shared meal."

"Julia Child?" she asked.

"Bruno Bettelheim," he said.

"You sure have a way with kids," she admonished.

"Don't you approve of cocktails?"

"Not for seventh graders."

"But he didn't want to be treated like a seventh grader. He wanted to be treated like a dude."

"He's a *kid*. Alcohol is illegal."

"Lots of good things are illegal. Oral sex is illegal in thirty states."

"That's not the point. Kids are not adults. They need limits. Rules."

"Who says?" he retorted. "Bucky Fuller, that cosmic guru, attributes his genius to never getting steamrolled by the system."

"I say, because I've got two kids to raise. And you'd say so, too, if you had some."

"The point is academic. I don't."

"You like them, though," she said.

"Sure, other people's to play with, then return."

"Like other people's wives?" she asked.

"Hey, wait a minute, how'd we get into this?" He reached for the wine bottle, frowned when he found it empty.

"Is that what you plan to do with me? Return me after the weekend?" she said, attempting levity. "You keep library books out longer than that."

He smiled. "Me and Alfred, we free spirits."

"And what am I?"

"You are a beautiful married lady, whom I am very lucky to be with."

"Who is going home to her husband tonight?" she asked.

"If that's what she wants."

"And you? What about you?"

"My way is winding. When the grant comes through,

I'll be in Thera. My life is that dig. That's not a home in the suburbs, a doctor husband, weekends at the club. With me, you wouldn't have any of it."

"Maybe I don't want it anymore."

"But maybe you do." He lifted her hair off her forehead, smoothed the vertical lines between her brows. "I think maybe you do."

A shiver, like a low voltage shock, ran the length of her spine. What was she doing and why? She felt dizzily disoriented. "We ought to get back," she said quickly. "The wind's come up." They gathered the remains of the picnic, handed them to a homeless man at the edge of the park and hailed a cab.

7

They returned to the hotel to find several messages in Ted's pigeonhole. Julia watched as he rummaged through the papers. "Something for you," he said, and handed her a sealed envelope. She thought of the Sokolovs, her heart racing as she tore it open. She'd been found out, denounced. Hurriedly, she skimmed the message, then sighed with relief. It was an advertisement from the hotel spa. Ted stood frowning at one of the messages. "It's a note from Torrance, the president of the society, confirming my presentation at five and a note from Roger and Cassandra advising me to cancel it."

"Why?" she asked.

"It's Cass playing oracle. 'The wolf is at your door, little piggie, take shelter in your brother's house.'" He jabbed the elevator button in a sharp tattoo. "Not by the hair of my chinny, chin, chin."

Julia kept her peace until they entered her hotel room, then ventured, "Maybe they know something."

"What could they possibly know? That Valanopolis is here from Athens to denounce me for being a bad boy and jumping the gun. But when he sees the reception this paper gets, and the grants start rolling in, that old fart will kiss my hand. If anything lifts that temple out of the sea it's going to be American technology, American know-how and American money. So not to worry. Time for a shower."

He flung his socks in one corner, his shoes in another, then looked up to see her unhook her bra. He watched as she rubbed the red elastic marks under her breasts, her vigorous movements causing her small high breasts to bob and jiggle. She caught his glance and stayed her hands.

"Don't stop," he urged, "I like it."

She grinned, then, cupping her breasts, ran the tip of her tongue across her parted lips.

"Fantastic," he said, sprawling across the bed, his eyes riveted to hers. "I'm yours."

Warming to the task, she gently flicked her nipples with her thumbs until they stiffened and flared. She laced her fingers at the back of her neck, arched her spine, ran her hands slowly, sinuously through her hair, tousling it over her eyes. She brought her hands coyly in front of her face, masking it, then opened her fingers like a shutter for a slow deliberate wink. A memory assailed her, of how she would decorously turn her back to Mark when she undressed. He liked looking at her body, but somehow she had always felt shy about being observed. Yet she loved theater. That's why she had chosen to teach it. With Ted that playful, dramatic side was being released. An aspect she barely knew she had.

"Just a minute," Ted said, checking his watch. "Yes, we have time." He spun the radio dial past news, sports and acid rock until he found a gentle India raga.

He plucked two scarves from her suitcase, tied one around her waist, the other as a veil around her head. He lay back upon the bed, naked, regal as a pasha, three pillows beneath his head, his penis already throbbing and lifting.

"Good evening, ladies and gentlemen," she intoned. "Welcome to *American Idol*. Keep your eyes peeled on our applause meter—" gingerly, she tweaked the top of his penis "—and discover which one of our contestants will be our lucky winner tonight. I shall play them all," she declared, "all those parts I've never gotten to play. Scheherazade, Mata Hari, Cleopatra…courtesans, houris, femme fatales." She turned the music up a notch louder and began to dance in a swaying, sinuous circle around the bed, slow pelvic thrusts and rolls punctuated by breast and shoulder shimmies. She cast off her body scarf, dancing naked but for her face veil; bending and twirling so that the corners of her scarf trailed along his body, grazing the applause meter, threatening to send it prematurely over the top. Her own body was afire with excitement, but she kept up the tantalizing play. She was one with the music, her dancing hypnotic and trancelike, the space between them charged with desire. She played with the delicious tension like a child wiggling a loose tooth that hung by a single thread. The music rose in crescendo; she whirled furiously, fingers raised to fling aside the last veil when the music cut to a sonorous male voice asking with oily concern, "Do you, like millions of others, suffer from occasional irregularity?"

She tumbled into bed, laughing, and wrapped her legs around Ted like a cobra. They made slow moist love without his ever lifting the last veil. When they untangled, the late afternoon sunlight striped the bed in moving bars of sun and shadow. Julia lay, watching the changing patterns, with Ted's head on her breast. "When I was a little girl," she said, "we had a fake fireplace that cast shadows like flames. I used to lie on the rug, watch them and dream."

He nuzzled at her breast, brushing its curve with parted lips. "Am I your fake flame?" he asked, guiding her hand to his belly.

"You are my real shadow," she answered.

He moaned as she caressed him with her fingertips. "Before your very eyes, the shadow is changing shape."

She watched as his cock stirred and stiffened. "Jung says our shadow is the part of ourselves that we fear and reject. The part that, in order to be whole, we must accept and integrate."

"So is that what I am, your shadow side? Your red-bearded devil?"

"My impulsive side, my adventurous, daring side," she said, rolling his penis between her palms.

"Your carnal side," he said, as he helped her to settle astride his belly. He moaned as she slipped him inside her. "You're the sexiest lady I've had in years."

"You release it in me," she said as she rotated her hips like a corkscrew, grinding her clitoris across his pelvic bone so that its flame transfused her body. She pumped her desire nearly to the breaking point, then paused, lingering at the precipice, weightless and balanced, watching his hands milk her breasts, watching the rhythmic circling of their hips, watching Ted's flushed face, his bared teeth, his wild eyes.

She slid off and, kneeling between his legs, took his

stiff cock into her mouth. She sipped the clear drops from his foreskin, ran her tongue over his silky length, then opened her mouth and filled it with his throbbing fullness. She licked and sucked until she felt her uterus begin to contract, then she heightened her pace and pressure until Ted came in her mouth, moaning and crying her name. He tasted of the sea and she swallowed the spray. In all her years with Mark, despite his begging and bullying, she had refused to do this. But with Ted she had sought it. Some barrier had been crossed, she knew that. But why now? And why with this man?

They showered together, soaping and scrubbing each other assiduously. Ted lathered her hair and massaged her scalp until it tingled. They dried and powdered each other's rosy skin. After Ted left for his own room to dress, Julia brushed her dark hair and studied herself in the mirror. In a few years, she thought, there would be wrinkles and crow's-feet, bags and droops and purple veins. But not yet. Now, her color high from lovemaking, her eyes sparkling, she looked young and vibrant. She unearthed the best lingerie she'd brought, slipped into a moss-green silk sheath and high-heeled sandals, silver necklace and earrings, then knocked on the door of Ted's room.

He was magnificent, lean and straight in a perfectly tailored blue pin-striped suit, pristine white shirt, Hermès silk tie, his hair and beard brushed to perfection.

When he smiled at her admiration, his teeth shone strong and white against his full red mouth. He was dazzling, strong and virile and powerfully made; given a trident he could be Poseidon himself.

"You are going to knock them dead," she said softly.

"It's all in here," he said, holding up a thick manila folder. "Foolproof. Every step of the way. The slides will document the correlation of the *Critias* with the findings on Thera. Then I'll show a spreadsheet of the cost of the dredging operation to reclaim the temple. When the society sanctions the paper, the funding will be in the bag. Tonight is going to change history."

"Are you nervous?" she asked.

He held the manila envelope in one hand, the black box in the other. "Excited, yes. Nervous, no. Let Valanopolis be nervous. Tonight I steal his thunder."

As they entered the elevator, she asked, "Do you want to go in by yourself? I could go later." In answer, he closed his fingers around hers. She could feel the dampness on his palm. The elevator doors opened to a deserted corridor, carpeted in gold squares.

"Follow the yellow brick road," she said.

"What am I lacking?" he asked. "Courage, a brain or a heart?"

"You've got more than enough courage and brains," she said. "And you've won my heart."

"But you're taking it home to Kansas?"

"Maybe?" she whispered. "Let's see what the wizard says."

"What wizard?"

"The inner one," she said.

The first person they saw as they entered the Redwood Room was Roger, filling his cup from a silver coffee urn. The room was buzzing with milling forms, most of them men in tweed jackets, bespectacled, carrying clipboards and conversing loudly in a babble of languages. Roger gestured toward the black case Ted held. "What's in there, Teddy boy—banknotes?"

"After you see what's in here, money won't be a problem."

"Well, on the slim chance that you're right, your triumph will be well recorded." Roger gestured toward the television cameras, the row of newsmen. "And if not, a scientific cockfight might be colorful." He placed his arm around Ted's shoulders, drawing him back toward the wall, his body shielding their conversation. "The abstract of the correlation between Atlantis and Thera as Bronze Age cultures is interesting," Roger began. "All the evidence from Akrotiri—the villas, the frescoes—is good stuff, but the scheme to excavate the caldera is crazy. To dig half a mile into silt and rock for a figment of Plato's imagination, for a temple that never was, for a god that was unknown in that culture, is insane."

Roger's face softened as he ran his fingers lightly over his brother's arm. "You remember that summer at Jones Beach when you talked Mother into buying you a metal detector? You spent every day for two months running that damn pole over the sand, churning up beer cans and bottle caps and hairpins. I went swimming and played ball and you looked for treasure. There wasn't any treasure."

"There is now," Ted said, hoisting the case. "It just took me a while to find it."

Roger's eyebrows rose in a skeptical arch, but he nodded and smiled at Julia. "Come what may, I'll meet you in the lobby tonight at eight." He walked off to join Cass who, draped in chiffon tie-dye, was holding forth on UFOs to a short bald man who seemed far more interested in the flight patterns of her untethered breasts. Several middle-aged men came over to greet Ted and were dutifully introduced as Professor Xanthas, Dr. Schmelling and Mr. Campbell, later identified as "the bastard who fired me from Yale, a megalomaniac with a squad of graduate slaves and a brilliant curator, who really knows his Minoan." Ted scanned the room.

"Is Valanopolis here?" Julia asked.

"I don't see him yet, but he's not easily missed. I'll

show you what I mean." Ted fished out a picture from his wallet of himself and another man on the deck of a ship. Both wore bathing trunks and scuba tanks; Ted's companion stood a head taller and was barrel-chested, with a shock of white hair and the bearing and imperious stare of an emperor.

Ted returned the picture to his wallet. "If Val shows, he shows. I know he's angry. I've jumped the gun. He wanted to handle the publicity in his own way. First the exhaustive dig report, then the cautious scholarly journal, then a discreet professional conference and finally the popular press revealing only the facts, no speculations. Hell, he doesn't even want the name Atlantis used. He hit the ceiling when I leaked the preliminary reports on the underwater canals. Wants the whole project called 'Site 44: Report on a Minoan Bronze Age Culture.' Doesn't that have a poetic ring! The power is in the name Atlantis. Once we find the temple, the money will come pouring in. We'll be able to excavate the whole city, the shops, the houses, the bullrings. It will make Pompeii look like Peoria."

The society chairman, a portly man with a toupee, beckoned to Ted as he read the introduction. "Our next paper on Excavation of Site 44, Thera, Greece, is presented by Theodore Gustafson, research assistant to Professor Achilles Valanopolis, Chief of Antiquities, Archeological Institute of Greece."

As Ted stepped up to the podium, a corona of flashbulbs ignited, a camera whirred and a group of newsmen moved closer. Julia took a seat in the back row, near Roger and Cass, and watched as Ted settled his papers on the podium, handed a cartridge of slides to the projectionist, then, reaching into his inner jacket pocket, removed a pair of horn-rimmed glasses. She had not seen him wear them before. They blanketed his roguish eyes and gave him a controlled, scholarly mien. It was strange to reconcile the animal romp of an hour ago with his current blue-suited dignity. She thought of Mark, who in the early years of their marriage, when interrupted in their lovemaking by a patient's late night phone call, had kept his fingers on her nipple while his voice ministered and prescribed. They had made a lot of love in those years.

Ted leaned his elbows on the podium and slowly scanned his audience. "From time to time in the history of humankind, men—and learned men at that—have entertained themselves in contemplating insoluble riddles." His voice was as measured and rich as the beginning of a fairy tale. "They have wondered what song the sirens sang? How many angels could dance on the head of a pin? What was the formula for transmuting base metal into gold?" He paused dramatically. "Among these conundrums was the tantalizing riddle of the lost island of Atlantis. Did it exist? If so, where and when? And most importantly, will we ever be able to find it?

"Men have sought the fabled Atlantis in every ocean from the Sargasso Sea to the coast of Bermuda. Indeed it has been said that if all the theories on Atlantis could be collected, one would have a very good historical contribution to our knowledge of human insanity."

The laughter of agreement rippled through the audience. Ted was like a magician, Julia thought, fumbling his cards the first time to build suspense.

Ted waited until the murmuring stilled. "Today I will prove to you, beyond a shadow of a doubt," he proclaimed, his voice rising with excitement, "that Atlantis truly existed. It exists today. At the bottom of the Aegean Sea. Buried in the caldera of Thera. Waiting to be discovered. Ladies and gentlemen, I give you Plato's lost city of Atlantis. First slide, please."

With a dramatic sweep, the lights in the auditorium dimmed and the screen was flooded with the image of a dramatic fresco. In a scene of tumbling action, a supple, bronzed-skinned athlete vaulted backward over the back of an enormous black bull, while a fair-skinned maiden in bracelets and loincloth waited to catch him as he bounded back to earth.

"This fresco of bull vaulting is from the east wing of the Palace of Knossos on the island of Crete, circa 1500 B.C.," Ted explained. "It is perhaps the best known artifact of the Minoan culture. The bull cult was widespread in Minoan art and religion." Two slides flashed simultaneously upon the screen: a large pair of bull's horns surmounting a doorway, then a drinking vessel shaped like a bull's head. "The fresco you have just seen is from Crete," Ted said. "The sacerdotal horns and vessel are from Thera. I propose to show that Plato's Royal City is Crete and Plato's Ancient Metropolis is Thera." He paused for effect. "I propose to show beyond the shadow of a doubt that Thera is Atlantis!"

In the silence, a richly accented voice boomed out of the darkness. "Atlantis is a cautionary tale developed by Plato to teach the Greeks the value of moderation, to warn them of the pitfalls of greed and overweening ambition. And to judge from today's presentation it is still a useful story." The speaker paused for the rising riffle of laughter. "Atlantis, my learned colleagues," he continued, "is a myth, a fiction, a fantasy, a fit subject for Aesop or Boccaccio. It has nothing to do with the excavations on Thera, it only obfuscates, confuses, leads away vital investigative energies from the real and measurable into the miasma of make-believe."

Somewhere in the midst of Valanopolis's speech, the lights had come on, and when he finished, the large man stood, arms akimbo, directly in front of the podium. The audience was electric with excitement. As Julia scanned their waiting faces she could glimpse the suppressed smiles, see the glinting amused eyes. Two scientists behind her dissected the situation, the older one supplying the facts. "Gustafson is the enfant terrible of the profession, rode that Atlantis hobby horse of his right out of tenure at Yale and a chance to head up their Mediterranean digs."

"I hear he financed the Thera expedition on family money," the younger man snickered.

"Absolutely! Even Valanopolis couldn't refuse all that fancy equipment. The old boy's no fool. They don't call him the Badger for nothing."

"Why the Badger?" the younger man asked.

"The Badger, dear boy, is very helpful on digs, he burrows toward soft ground. Follow him and you get to the goods."

"So what went wrong?" the other asked.

"Apparently a difference of opinion as to what constituted the goods," the older man chuckled. "Pull out your umbrella, sweetheart, this promises to be juicy."

Ted waited for the room to quiet, then calmly announced, "I wish to thank Professor Valanopolis for his valuable dissent. I trust that he will grant me and this august body the benefit of further dialogue directly following my presentation. Next slide, please."

To Julia's relief, Valanopolis resumed his seat and the lights were once again dimmed. Ted had regained control. She watched as his slides flowed over the screen like a light show at a rock concert, the myriad colors and shapes dancing to the rhythm of his voice. Frescoes depicting scenes of daily life on the sunlit island 3,500 years ago: two pigtailed boys boxing with single gloves, a group of maidens on a flower-strewn riverbank. Julia recognized the girls' familiar rouged nipples, recalled her own and the subsequent lovemaking. She felt a warm diffused glow, then a rapid stab of regret. Soon she would only have the memory to spice her orderly days and warm her barren nights. She studied Ted's face, trying to imprint it in her mind, the full curve of his lower lip above the flaming beard, the wry beginnings of a smile. Her rustling sigh was so audible it caused Roger's head to turn.

She needed Eros; she could no longer live without it, no longer stifle the desires of her body, the yearnings of her soul. And yet how could she hurt Mark? He had been a dutiful husband, stood by her, supported her through good times and bad. He had been faithful, responsible, attentive. And once there had been love. She remembered the early years of their marriage, the long weekends when the world revolved about them. That sweet discovery stage when every love song seemed true. They had built a home and a family together. How could she hurt her children? Uproot their lives? Tear everything they knew and loved apart? Other women left their marriages. It was seldom easy but they did it. They made a decision and committed to it, wholeheartedly, not looking back.

She needed to choose. Make it work. But how? And what?

Julia was so lost in her thoughts that she didn't hear the altercation when it first began. She startled, almost as if wakened from a dream, to hear Valanopolis's voice ring out.

"….an academic disgrace. A total fallacy. Mr. Gustafson's ridiculous claims depend on his supposition that Plato's Temple of Poseidon is submerged in the caldera of Thera. There is no such temple for the very simple reason that Poseidon, the god of the sea, was completely unknown to the Minoans of Thera. What we have in the story of Atlantis is Plato superimposing his own religious beliefs on an ancient myth. Atlantis exists in the imagination alone, just like every other utopian vision. There was no temple, there were no golden statues…there was…no Poseidon." Valanopolis resumed his seat with the grim mien of a man who had issued a distasteful but necessary order of execution.

Amidst the murmurings in the hall, Julia heard the young scientist's voice. "He's right! You don't have to be a classicist to know the Poseidon information. What a gaffe. What's Gustafson trying to pull? No wonder he was thrown out of Yale."

Ted was beginning to speak; Julia leaned forward, straining to hear him through the men's continuing chatter. Ted's face was flushed, his jaw clenched. She feared for him, her stomach knotting the way it did when she watched Davey play basketball, racing down the court bouncing the ball furiously in front of him, dodging the oncoming team, evading the snatching hands. Davey wore that same look of inner fire, as if his face were a translucent lantern. Within the frenzied action, Davey would seem to float in stillness. And she, as well, so fused was she with his drive, his intensity. And if she could, she would have sent that sphere sailing through the hoop for him, would have become that sphere, that hoop, if she could help him win.

Ted was holding aloft a black leather case, the same one he had carried on the plane. The same one with which he had lured her to the conference. Now its contents would be revealed.

"It is quite true," Ted began, "as Doctor Valanopolis has

postulated that there are, as of yet, no extant Minoan artifacts in the likeness of Poseidon. Indeed, we have only found statues of beardless men. Poseidon, as we know him from the Greeks, was always bearded. However, we may speculate that since none of the Minoan men were bearded, as evidenced by their frescoes and drawings, that their gods, conceived in the image of their worshippers, were likewise without beards. So, then, how are we to recognize the great sea god, Poseidon, if not by his beard? Perhaps by his other ever-present symbol, the trident? Nowhere in Minoan excavations have we found a trident. Hence we have assumed that to those great seafarers, those skilled sailors who controlled the Mediterranean, the great sea god Poseidon was unknown. But we would be mistaken. He was not unknown, ladies and gentlemen, merely undiscovered."

With the deftness of a magician, Ted flicked open the box, whisked off a black velvet drape and revealed a marble bust of a square-jawed man holding aloft a marble shaft whose tip ended in three clearly defined prongs. The revelation of the bust caused an audible, contagious stir of wonder in the audience, a rising swarm of voices, a whir of cameras. Ted placed the statue on the podium, firmly supporting it with both hands. His face was weary, benevolent, like the champion heavyweight saluting the bloodied contender.

"It is through the generosity of Professor Valanopolis that I am able to show the Poseidon head to you today, for it was in his dig, trench 39, pit D-4, Akrotiri that I uncovered it. I wish to thank him formally now. I give you Professor Valanopolis, Chief of Antiquities, Athens, Greece."

Valanopolis rose to his feet and stood silently acknowledging the applause. Something in his implacable stance, the stern set of his lips worried Julia.

"We have a saying in my country, count no man lucky until the end," Valanopolis began. "Sometimes our good fortune may vanish in an instant, destroyed when we see the whole picture. And today we will see the whole picture of this so-called Poseidon and his trident." With the slow solid tread of a pallbearer he walked up the aisle carrying two rolled-up scrolls beneath his arm. He stood patiently while a rattled chairman produced masking tape to affix them to the wall.

Julia waited, digging her fingernails into the soft flesh of her palms, a way of warding off pain by self-inflicting it that she had mastered in the dentist's chair while awaiting the first jab of the drill. She feared for Ted and was helpless to intervene.

Valanopolis extracted a laser pointer from his jacket pocket and pointed to the scroll on the right. It was an enlarged photograph of Ted's Poseidon, blind stare and standing trident. On the left was the identical bust, but instead of the trident there was an upraised arm, and at the end of it a hand, palm pointed outward. The thumb and the little finger had been drawn in dotted lines as if they had broken away. The remaining three fused digits formed Ted's trident. Julia unclenched her fists; felt her body sag. There was no longer a need to pay attention. It was seen at a glance, the same way so many sorrows are instantaneously glimpsed...the indifference in a lover's eye, the mark of a prowler on the rug, the swerving wheel of an oncoming car.

She observed with detachment the showing of a series of slides, three similar busts, all with out-turned palms, one from the archives of the Archeological Museum of Athens, one from the storehouse of the Metropolitan, one from the basement of the British Museum, all Minoan or Mycenean. "All available to Mr. Gustafson," Valanopolis added, "had he but chosen to do a bit of scholarly research before precipitously making his discovery known to the world."

"I would not wish to make my case on analogy alone," continued Valanopolis. "My colleagues and I have further explored trench 39, pit D-4 and found the following shards, pieced them together and discovered one digit that fits perfectly onto Mr. Gustafson's bust." A slide flashed on the screen of the marble thumb in place. "It's my pleasure to give the finger to Mr. Gustafson's Poseidon."

There was a wave of derisive laughter.

Valanopolis cut the laughter with a decorous cough. "Young men are, by nature, hasty, in a great rush to seek out information even when it proves self-destructive. We Greeks know well of this. Our own Oedipus was perhaps the first. A great tragedy. In the case of Mr. Gustafson, we have a similar catastrophe. For in his haste, not only has his scholarship been impugned, but I am afraid so has his freedom. He has committed an action both immoral and illegal—he has removed an antiquity from the country of origin without government permission. I will return the bust to the museum at Akrotiri immediately, but as for Mr. Gustafson, I am afraid that as minister of antiquities I must levy a severe fine and a suspension of excavating privileges. I regret that such a promising career has been sacrificed for a foolish fairy tale."

There was another whir of cameras, this time aimed at Valanopolis. Fewer though, Julia noted. An academic debunking wasn't as good a story as a golden temple resurrected from the sea. The scientists rose, stretched their legs, cracked their knuckles, shook their heads over the sad spectacle and went off in search of their wives and a stiff drink.

Julia stood against the back wall, watching while the last of the audience left. She surveyed the wreckage: crumpled papers, overturned chairs, paper coffee cups, abandoned pens. She and Ted were alone in the midst, like the unfortunate hosts of a party that had failed. She felt a wry impulse to tidy up, to straighten the furniture, sponge the stains off the upholstery, run the vacuum over the rug. So much planning, so much effort, so many bright hopes. And the guests hadn't liked it. There would be no reciprocal invitations. Nor would they come again.

She was assailed with conflicting emotions. A flood of pity and compassion for Ted, yet a troubling thread of doubt. Had he brought this upon himself through impetuosity, through sloppy scholarship? She thought of Mark's meticulous research and careful checking and re-checking of his medical diagnoses. And not for the first time she wondered about the line between spontaneity and irresponsibility.

Julia watched as Roger walked swiftly down the aisle toward Ted, who was filing slides back into a metal box. Ted looked up, saw Roger and shook his head, trying to stop him from approaching, but Roger paid no mind. He drew nearer with his hands open, palms up, the way one would approach an excitable animal. Ted's head shot up, his mouth a snarl. "Get the hell out of here. You got what you came for." Roger continued to approach, talking in a calm, soft voice, his murmurings interspersed by Ted's angry retorts until gradually Ted quieted and became still. Julia saw Roger's hand slowly rise and light upon his brother's shoulder. It rested there for a moment, motionless, shielding. As he left, Roger turned to Julia. "You're not going to leave him now, are you?" he asked. "He needs you."

Julia waited in silence as Roger departed. What should she do? It was nearly seven. She needed to leave for the airport very soon. What did Ted want? Need? When she was hurt or embarrassed, she wanted to hide, to disappear. No touch, no sympathy, no encouraging homilies. She wanted to burn in the shame, exorcising it with self-condemnation. Mark, on the other hand, following failure, wanted solace, justification that he was right. But Ted? What did Ted want? She realized how little she knew about him.

She caught his eye as he strode up the aisle, briefcase in one hand, slide box in the other. She fell in beside him and they walked in silence down the hall, into the elevator, watched the numbers flash till eight. Once in his room, he immediately poured them each a generous Scotch, then opened the drapes on the setting sun burnishing the Transamerica Pyramid. He took a long swallow of his drink, loosened his tie, kicked off his shoes, collapsed onto the bed. "That sneaky bastard," he said.

Then, beginning to smile, he added, "That slimy coot." His smile grew wider. "He did me one better." Ted slapped his thigh and laughed out loud. "The Old Badger lies like a thief and comes off looking like the Pope."

"What did he lie about?" she asked.

"That slide he showed of the missing fingers. It's a fraud. He never found a missing finger."

"How do you know?"

"Because I found it first."

"What?" she cried.

He grinned at her. "Don't look so shocked. They were in shards. I didn't know they were fingers. They could have been anything. I was digging in the new trench, and it gave way, maybe forty feet. I saw the bust gleaming like a full moon in all that ash. I threw a rope and climbed down. I swear to you when I saw the arm, I was sure it was a trident. Damn it, I dug it out with my hands and I burst into tears. Then next to it, I saw the fragments; they could have been fingers. They could have been anything. They had been broken in the fall, scattered…smashed."

"What did you do with them?"

"Dust thou art, to dust returneth."

"You destroyed them?"

He shook his head. "I couldn't. I'm an archeologist." He reached into his pocket, withdrew a small canvas sack, rattled it in his fist like a pair of dice.

"You've been carrying them all along!" she cried.

He spilled the marble fragments onto the desk, raked them with his fingers. "That old badger with his white hair and thunderbolt delivery, they all believed him. He draws in some dotted lines, adds a hunk of unidentified marble and throws me out of Greece." Ted downed the rest of his Scotch, turned on the TV and sat with his back to it, one leg thrown over a chair. Like Davey, Julia thought, stereo or TV as necessary accompaniment to conversation. "You know how that bastard managed to excavate Aghia Triada when the money dried up? Sucking up to the English. How do you think that Minoan statue got into the British Museum? Anything as long as he had the money to dig. Some conscience. Some morality." He looked up at Julia, who was still clasping her untouched glass. "Drink up," he said. "It's not over yet."

"Isn't it? You'll never be able to go back to Greece."

"That was just a family fight. I jumped the gun, wasn't careful enough, scientifically exacting enough. I took a leap of faith. Made it what I wanted it to be. Discounted the rest. It was a mistake." He lifted his head, meeting her eyes. "But the temple isn't a mistake. Believe me, Julia, it's real. Yet how do I convince them of that?"

"'In the middle of my life,'" she said, "'I found myself in a dark wood and knew not which way to go.'"

He looked at her questioningly.

"Dante," she said. *"The Divine Comedy."*

He rested his head against her breast. "Is that what this is?" he murmured. "Or is it *Paradise Lost?*"

Gently she stroked his hair and temples. Her fingers slid along his cheek, and to her surprise, she encountered wetness. She tilted his face upward and saw that his eyes were brimming. "Oh, sweetie," she murmured, and drew him close. And something in the softness of her voice, in her entering into and sharing of his sorrow, released his tears.

"I screwed up," he said. "Big-time." As she held him she was visited by memories of her own sorrows and those of others, always different yet always the same—lost pride, lost hope, lost love. Without intending to, she cried with him, her body an extension of his, her breathing linked with his. After a while, their tears stopped as they had begun, without transition, brief as a tropical storm. They lay stretched out upon the bed, their bodies entwined as light and empty as after lovemaking.

"You'd better go," he said. "Or you'll miss your plane."

She sat up, straightening her clothes. "Are you sure you're going to be all right?"

"I'll be fine."

"I wish I could stay."

"Me, too."

"But we'll keep in touch, right? This isn't just a…"

"No, it isn't," he said. "Not for me."

"Not for me, either," she said. Then what is it? she thought. How would she know? She needed more time. But how to get it? She couldn't call Mark again. Couldn't lie again. And yet she wanted so much to stay. The question she had been harboring for years, the question she had traveled all the way to Greece to ask, the question she had posed to the oracle at Delphi was burning inside her right now. The question that needed to be answered if she were to live her life fully. What about my marriage? Do I stay or do I go?

The ringing of the telephone interrupted her thoughts. It was the concierge.

"Mrs. Simon, you ordered a taxi to the airport?"

"I'll be right down," she said.

"Well, ma'am, you might want to call the airline. San Francisco airport is completely fogged in. I doubt there will be any planes leaving tonight."

Julia hung up the phone. Was it a sign? An omen? An oracular message? Or a mere coincidence, signifying nothing more than a random change in the weather? One thing was certain—it was a reprieve, albeit temporary. Under Ted's watchful eye, she dialed Mark's medical answering service and left a brief message. "This is Mrs. Simon, the doctor's wife. Please tell him my flight is delayed because of weather and that I'll be home tomorrow."

8

They rode to Mill Valley in Roger's vintage Mercedes convertible. Julia snuggled close to Ted in the back seat; the cool damp wind whipping across their faces made conversation impossible. The fog that had delayed her flight had not drifted as far as the Marin hills and the jeweled frame of the Golden Gate Bridge sparkled under the light of the full moon. Roger and Cass lived on the top of Mount Tamalpais, one of the three mountains sacred to the California Indians, in a sprawling A-frame whose cathedral windows looked out upon the city and Bay on one side and a eucalyptus grove on the other.

The former owner was a psychiatrist, Roger told them, and the house had been a meeting place for the luminaries of the Human Potential Movement. Gregory Bateson, Fritz Perls, Allan Watts, R.D. Laing and even the elusive Carlos Casteneda had smoked and slept and soaked here. The house still bore the dated trappings of a hippie pad. There were flokati rugs on the floors, tie-dyed spreads, hanging ferns and macramé, a water bed with a fake fur spread, rattan hammocks, and a conversation pit lined with black velvet.

Cass greeted them clad in OshKosh B'Gosh overalls that flashed the sides of her naked breasts each time she turned. Roger shed his shearling coat to reveal a multi-zippered jumpsuit. He mixed four towering mai tais, puckishly dusting the tops with geranium petals plucked from a table arrangement. He and Cass kept the conversation flowing, avoiding the debacle of the conference as if it were a fatal disease. There was no remonstrance of how one should have lived a cleaner life or consulted professional help earlier. The malignancy had been removed, indeed was now resting in Valanopolis's suitcase, but the patient's professional life was over. So what was there to do but eat, drink and distract.

Roger zipped open the front of his jumpsuit to scratch at the gray fuzz on his chest. "You're probably wondering about Ellie," he said to Ted. "Usual story. A midlife crisis. Male menopause. I had to change something. I didn't know what, so I changed everything. I left the marriage, the job, the house, the boat and the country club. I got a hair transplant, contact lenses, spent a month at an ashram. First workshop was 'The Body Can Do Anything,' the second was 'The Mind Can Do Anything.' Guess which one I met Cass in?"

Julia admired the swing of Cass's plump breasts beneath the striped bib of the overalls. She suppressed a giggle; the rum was getting to her. "The Mind."

"That's right," Roger said, nodding with pleasure. "You know Cass is a gifted psychic. She scored highest in the group in remote viewing, clairvoyance and precognition."

"But I flunked tele...tele...telekenisis," Cass said with a smile, her slurred speech suggesting that she was several mai tais ahead of her guests. She ran a long red fingernail down the V of Roger's exposed chest. "I have trouble affecting inanimate objects like bending keys and lifting tables. But," she said reflectively, threading her finger through his zipper loop, "I can make some things move." She unzipped Roger's jumpsuit a bit farther, exposing his tanned belly. "I'm hopeless with metal," she said, "but I seem to have a way with flesh."

Roger laughed delightedly and Julia joined him. It was funny, audacious. Encouraged, Cass slipped her hand inside the opening; Julia watched Cass's fingers disappear into the denimed space, then after a slow companionable grope, emerge. Julia felt a flush rise to her face. Confused, embarrassed, yet curiously aroused, she sought Ted. He stood by the window gazing out into the starry night. She joined him and leaned her head against his shoulder. His arm encircled her and she breathed deeply of his scent, citrus and musk. Whenever it would waft across her world again, she thought, she would be assailed by memory. By memory and loss. Together they watched a plane drift across the sky, the white lights flicker and fade.

"I'll be on one of those tomorrow," she said.

"Only if you want to be."

"I have to be."

He leaned forward, pressing his forehead against the cool glass. "Death and taxes. Those are the only certainties. The rest is choice."

"But I have a home, a family."

She could feel the turn of Cass's head at the mention of family. Strange that they should choose this time to talk of it. Almost as if they needed an audience for which to stage the drama of their lives; an audience to gasp and sigh and dab at their eyes, to shout "author" and throw roses. Adultery and Atlantis. Sex comedy with a classical touch. Playing now in illicit trysts across the nation. Working premise: when there is marriage without love, there is love without marriage.

"Stay with me," he said.

"What?"

"I want you. Stay with me."

"Another day or two won't make it any easier," she said.

"Stay for good," he said.

"For good?" she repeated. She felt her breath catch in her throat. It would be wonderful. But it was impossible. Wasn't it? Then quickly, not giving him a chance to answer, she leavened it, using the language of long-past childhood games. "You mean for keeps. No backsies. No tradesies. No do-overs."

His hands tightened about her shoulders. "I'm falling in love with you. I don't want this to end."

Nor do I, she thought, this exhilaration of the flesh that explodes all day long in starbursts of joy, like those cold-capsule ads on TV, providing round-the-clock protection from boredom, lassitude, aging, meaninglessness. Maybe it would someday grow to include compassion, empathy and understanding, all those things she had once hoped for with Mark. But meanwhile, she had this—an exultation of the flesh, a miraculous, magical celebration of the body. This discovery! But could it be sustained? She thought of Valanopolis's meticulous piecing together of pot shards, in contrast to Ted's precipitous leap into the sea. Was Ted capable of such perseverance?

"You could join me in Greece," he said. "Or I could come to L.A. Whatever's right."

"Nothing's right," she said.

"Then whatever's operable," he amended.

Julia was stunned into silence. She knew how strong her attraction to Ted was, but until this moment she hadn't realized the feelings were mutual, reciprocated. Things had changed radically. Now what?

"Hey, you two," Roger said, "quit the private talks. It's a party, right?" He ambled over, took each of them by the hand and led them to a black leather sofa. "Now look what Daddy has brought you." Gleefully, he opened a soft leather pouch, spilled some of the dark tobacco upon the marble coffee table. Then, scooping a mound in his fingers, he stuffed it into the bowl of a rainbow-colored glass pipe. "Acapulco gold," he said, "mellow yellow." He lit the grass, inhaled deeply, drove the smoke down into his lungs, held it there for a long moment, then exhaled, sighed with pleasure and passed the pipe first to Cass, then to Ted. The weed smelled sweet and aromatic, redolent of damp autumn leaves trod underfoot. Julia awaited her turn. She had never smoked marijuana before, refusing it at college parties. She was too straight. Too fearful of getting caught. Of losing control. Was she now experiencing a delayed adolescence? Or was she simply ready for it? When the pipe came to her, she puffed dutifully, filling her mouth with the smoke, then releasing it in a dense cloud.

"You've got to inhale it, babe," Ted's said, his lips grazing her cheek.

"I can't get it down," she protested. "I've seen too many lung cancer commercials."

"There's no nicotine in grass," Ted said. "No irritants. Just peace and light."

"Pretend it's a snorkel tube," Cass coached. "Imagine you're swimming in a beautiful coral reef, watching the waving colors of the sea fans, the darting fish glimmering in the sunlight. You want to stay down and see all that gliding, glistening underwater life, but you need air. Your lungs need sweet life-giving air, so you suck in, suck in deep. Let it fill your lungs. Let it expand your vision."

Julia took a deep toke, held it for a moment, then exhaled, sputtering and coughing.

"Get a little water down your tube?" Ted said, laughing.

"Just swallow the smoke," Roger suggested. "You'll get enough by osmosis."

Roger filled the pipe again, passing it carefully around the circle as they interspersed their puffs with swigs of icy mai tais. As Julia waited her turn, she devoured the fruit first in her own glass and then in each of the others. "I'm starving," she said. "Do you have anything to eat?"

Cass left the room, then reappeared with a Loretta

Young flourish in the doorway, balancing a tray laden with pâté, cheese and ripe peaches. As Cass knelt to place the tray upon the low coffee table, one of her breasts slipped out from the side of her overalls. Roger reached up from his sprawled position on the rug and gently placed it back in its moorings.

To her surprise, Julia found the gesture endearing, not embarrassing at all. Was it the pot or her new appreciation for the sensual? Or both?

Cass watched as Julia reached for a large, downy peach. "Grass always makes you hungry. Hungry, horny and happy." She stayed Julia's hand. "Hey, hold on a second. I've got a great idea." She tossed each of the men a peach, taking one herself. She cradled the fruit in her hands. "Now do what I do. And don't laugh. It'll be a gas. I want you to become aware of your peach. Observe its shape. Its curves. Where it is full. Where it tapers. Its cleft. Its stem. Where it is hard. Where it is soft. Now close your eyes and rub it around your face, feel its temperature, its texture, inhale its perfume."

Julia giggled. "This is awfully sixties," she said. Nevertheless she felt her senses slowly suffuse with the essence of peach.

"Some parts of the sixties were great," Cass said. "Now very slowly, open your mouth and gently, tenderly enter your peach." As she continued to speak, her voice became deeper and more languid. "Feel your teeth break into its flesh, tear a small morsel free. Now slowly chew the peach, feel the juice fill your mouth, feel the pulp between your teeth, keep chewing until the fragment of peach is completely pulverized. Then and only then… swallow."

Julia chewed until the peach dissolved into velvety syrup, slipping in little bursts of summer sweetness down her throat, each taste new and exquisite, distinct and subtle as a musical note, the whole an intricate melody. Her senses vibrated. So much sensation in so small an object, hidden in wait for her awareness. Slowly, she bit another morsel of peach, savoring it, letting it dissolve against her tongue. Normally, in the same space of time, she would be picking at the denuded pit, searching for overlooked strands, still hungry, still unsatisfied. Maybe this was why the Slow Food Movement was taking hold. Savor the moment.

They had all eased to the white flokati rug now, sitting in a close circle, passing the pipe, sharing the last of the peaches. Julia's head lay against Ted's shoulder, her feet comfortably resting on Cass's curled knees. "Is it the pot that makes everything slow down?" she asked.

"It helps," Cass said, twirling strands of Roger's thinning red hair through her fingers, "but mostly it's just a change of perspective."

As Ted's hands stroked her neck and shoulders, Julia recalled the flight from Greece, her thigh warm against his. Remembered peering through the wispy clouds to the gray-green mountains below, like the gods gazing down from Mount Olympus upon a miniature world.

"We're all energy," Roger said, taking a last drag of the smoldering pipe. "All pulsating energy. Sometimes we're waves, sometimes we're particles. There is no beginning, no end. There is no time and space. Quantum physics tells us there is no longer cause and effect. Energy can neither be created nor destroyed. Reality is subjective. We can do anything—travel through time, through space, communicate with other planets. Our consciousness is boundless. We can be in two places at the same time."

Cass giggled. "Wouldn't you like to stay here in this room, Julia, and still be at home with your husband and kiddies?"

"It might solve some problems," Julia admitted.

"The good wife and mother can fly back to Los Angeles, cook dinner and tuck the kiddies into bed while Julia the Jolly balls in Mill Valley," Cass said

"Is that b-a-l-l or b-a-w-l?" Ted asked.

"Bald as in bean," Roger said, raising his head. "Do you think I need another transplant?"

"Maybe a heart transplant," Cass teased.

Ted's hands moved beneath the silky cloth of Julia's blouse, "Julia has a big heart, a big brave heart…and brave little breasts."

"Do you, Julia?" Cass asked. "Why are your breasts brave?"

"Because they stand up to be counted," Ted said. "They're firm and stalwart. And—" he paused, searching for the perfect phrase "—they meet you eye-to-eye."

"Show us," Cass said.

"Yes, we need to see," Roger said, "it's un-American to deny us examples of great courage. Think of Kennedy and the U-2 boat."

"George Washington and the cherry tree," Cass offered.

"Daniel Ellsberg, Barbara Fritchie…"

Julia retreated to the circle of Ted's arms. It was as if she owned this work of art and was selfishly refusing to unveil it.

Sensing Julia's discomfort, Cass intervened. "Cease and desist," she said. "We're going to take this matter to where it belongs. Follow me."

Cass led them through a sumptuous bedroom, furnished with a round platform bed, mirrored walls and ceiling. Glass doors opened upon a covered patio, nestled against the hill with rough stone walls, leafy ferns and a trickling stream to simulate a mountain grotto. In the center, surrounded by planters of daisies, stood a steaming hot tub flanked by two white leather massage tables. "Welcome to the Golden Door North," Cass said.

Ted, Roger and Cass shed their clothes swiftly and slipped into the tub. Julia fumbled with her buttons, trying to ignore Roger's interested appraisal. Before, she had been naked only to Mark, then to Ted, now to a stranger. Was he comparing her body to Cass's, finding it wanting beside Cass's concave belly and smooth thighs? Julia plunged in, then hurriedly sprang up again, skin red and steaming. "It's boiling," she yelped.

"You'll get used to it," Ted advised. "Ooze in slowly."

She sat upon the cool stone rim, dangling her feet, gradually submerging bit by bit. At last she was covered to her neck in the hot bubbling water. Taking her by the hand, Cass demonstrated the three Jacuzzi nozzles; one hit between her shoulder blades, another at her waist. "Get ready for the third!" Cass warned as she positioned Julia. The third aimed directly at the base of her spine and, when Julia turned around to face it, the warm pulsating jet delivered a powerful erotic massage. She gasped with pleasure.

"Beats a vibrator any day," Cass chortled. She then proceeded to press a button concealed beneath a fern, and the ceiling of the grotto rolled back to reveal the moon and starlit sky.

As Julia stared in openmouthed awe, Ted, moved by her delight, encircled her in his arms and drew her toward him. She lay, her head on his shoulder, her body resting on the surface, her hair floating behind her, suspended between earth and sky, balanced effortlessly, connected yet free. And all the weight of decisions, of commitments, of ambivalences drifted away. They lay together, almost dozing, until the heat grew too intense. Ted climbed out first and awaited her with a thick white towel. Humming softly, he patted her dry with slow circular movements. Her eyes half-closed, she was back in her mother's kitchen, the kitchen of her childhood.

She felt her legs dangling off her mother's soft lap, her wet hair splattering her mother's cotton housedress of pink rosebuds and green binding. Cradling was a special treat for a big girl of eleven, years too old for such holding. But this time she was recovering from a long spring illness and a high fever, finally well enough for a hair wash at the kitchen sink. Afterward, she remembered her mother untangling her hair with a wide-toothed comb, wincing in sympathy as she pulled the knots free, but it was sweet pain, a small price to be a lap baby again.

As Ted rubbed her temples and the nape of her neck, Julia purred like a cream-filled cat. She kissed his thumbs, placed her lips on the pulse beat of his wrist and breathed in rhythm to his heartbeat. He cupped his hand along the curve of her brow and carefully cleared away the wet tendrils.

She watched as the moonlight flashed diamonds in the droplets caught in his hair and beard. He was dazzling, his skin ruddy and smooth. She ran her fingers along the firm muscles of his legs, the curls of soft reddish hair that furred his body. His cock stirred and she felt a matching heat in her own groin; she wanted him inside her.

She felt a hand lightly touch her shoulder, move along the line of her breast and playfully tweak her already erect nipple. She turned. The hand had long red fingernails.

Julia glanced at Ted to gauge his reaction, but his face was benign, showing neither approval nor dismay. It was her scene, her decision. Another illumination—how often she would use Mark's disapproval as a springboard, like parental opinion, a sure mark to push against. She studied Ted again. Was there no judgment or had she not learned to read it yet? Would it come later, after she had chosen?

Ted moved her hand lower, to his rising erection. Her mind resisted, embarrassed and judgmental of public displays, but her hand caressed his velvet pulsing organ with pleasure. She traced the circle of his testicles, held the sweet swinging weight, felt the delicate papery skin, the swelling veins and rising pressure. He began a slow rumble of pleasure that echoed in her own throat. She felt Cass's soft hands slip gently around her shoulders, felt long tapered fingernails trace the hollows in her throat with the same rhythm, the same delicacy with which she was touching Ted. This mirror image was being traced on her neck and breasts, as if her own hand were caressing her the way she wanted to be caressed, but with an added amplified dimension.

It was so like the mirror exercise in improvisational acting, a perennial, like the barre exercises in ballet. Two students would face each other; one would lead, the other follow, simultaneously mirroring her partner's movement and expressions, neither predicting nor lagging behind.

Then the lead would shift; the one who had led became the follower. The focus would shift back and forth until a connection was forged, a blending of rhythms, a flow. Then the final direction was given: "No one lead, no one follow. Let the movement come from between you."

That was happening now. Julia's hand on Ted's body was moving in rhythm to Cass's hand on hers, the energy flowing in a rippling stream down their bodies. And the vision that came was that although it was Ted's chest she was stroking, it was to Cass that she was making love. It was Cass's breasts, Cass's mouth. And the image flowed out of the mirror and into the night, and she was in Cass's arms and her tongue was meeting Cass's tongue, and her nipples, taut and tiny, were rubbing against the other woman's chest. And her mouth was suckling, feeling the rosy roundness pressing on her nose, enveloping her in sweet cushioned flesh. She was both mother and infant. The love-play was delicate yet deep, new yet utterly familiar. For once Eros was engaged, Julia discovered, all flesh was one and the body reclaimed its animal nature. And she was awash in the pure delight of skin on skin. She surrendered to it, feeling soft and tender and drowsy. Her last thought before falling asleep was strange and unexpected. Could she feel this way with Mark?

Hours later, she awoke to the advent of dawn and a spectacular orange sun rising above the lifting San Francisco fog. Ted lay crumpled beside her, in the mirrored bedroom, snoring deeply. She didn't remember getting there from the hot tub. She closed her eyes again recalling last night, not sure how much had actually happened or how much she had dreamed. Lesbian fantasies were common—she remembered reading that. She had thought about it herself sometimes. And now she had experienced it. So many new experiences in such a short space of time. Not one she wanted or needed to have again, yet she didn't regret the incident. It was teaching her something valuable about her sensuality, about her desires and her limits.

Ted was red-eyed and sleep creased when she roused him, and together they slipped past the bedroom where Cass lay in sleep mask and earplugs. The running shower water announced Roger's whereabouts.

"Shouldn't we say goodbye?" she asked.

Ted shook his head, rummaged in her purse for a lipstick and scrawled upon the mirror. *Fun party. Thanks a bunch.* He called for a cab and they left with Roger still in the shower, working his way jubilantly through the score of *Hair.*

Back at the hotel, Julia stripped, turned on the shower as hot as she could stand, and stood beneath the spray. The memory of last night's hot tub incident rose in her mind.

She leaned back against the steamy tile of the shower and remembered being caressed with exquisite knowledge, with magical timing, with total attention by Cass. And Julia had opened herself to those caresses and returned them, discovering a newfound ability to give and receive. It was as if what she shared with Ted had freed that ability. She wondered if it were truly transferable. If when she returned to Mark, their lovemaking could benefit from this experience. Would she ever tell him about this weekend? She doubted it. How could she tell him and not hurt him? And yet there was something important for both of them that she longed to share.

Julia stepped out of the shower and discovered a large puddle on the floor from the deflected spray. She dutifully mopped it with a bath towel, wrung the excess water into the tub and hung up the towel to dry as if there were no maid, as if she were once again the keeper of the house, cleaning stray hairs from the sink, brushing talcum from the floor. She screwed the cap on the toothpaste, aligned the towels, rubbed the shower film from the full-length mirror. Dispassionately, she studied her reflection, her hair in wet clumps showing strands of gray, her skin blotchy red—dermographia, Mark called it—bearing the marks of her scrubbing, a slight stomach pouch despite her weight loss. Everything needed shaving or plucking. No Aphrodite there. And yet she felt remarkably at peace with her image. She paused, resting her cheek on the cool glass, heard Ted's footsteps behind her.

"Hey you, how are you feeling?" His finger merged the droplets on her bare back to one thin line. "No postcoital depression?"

"Postorgy depression," she corrected.

"A little fooling around doesn't constitute an orgy."

"What do you call it then?"

"Partying?" he suggested.

"Sounds horrible, like those creeps who can't get laid anyplace but the Sexual Freedom League."

"It was just an evening, Julia. We had a couple of drinks, smoked some weed, cavorted in the hot tub and went home. It didn't mean anything."

"It did to me."

He kissed the back of her neck. "First time?"

She nodded.

"We don't have to do it again," he said.

"It was okay, once. I was curious, but it wasn't like it is with us."

"We are of a different order." He faced her, his eyes locking with hers, and their joined gaze lit her body like a giant klieg light. Yet that light would be turned off soon and it would be a cold dark night without it.

"So...what happens now?" she asked.

"How about breakfast?" he said.

"That's not what I meant."

"I know," he said. "What happens, Julia my sweet, is whatever we want to happen."

"It's not that easy," she said.

"It's about choice," he said. "Choosing to be together."

"But I chose to be with Mark," she said.

"And you can choose not to be with him."

"And then will I choose not to be with you?"

"Or I with you? Could be," he said.

"Then what lasts?"

"What's so good about lasting?" he said. "Ice cream melts. Wine evaporates. Logs burn. They're meant to be used."

"But people aren't disposable," she argued.

"Then what are we doing with all those cemeteries?" He reached for a towel and blotted her back and shoulders. "The trouble with you is you never sowed your wild oats."

"When I was a teenager, I was obsessed with sex," she declared.

His glance was quizzical.

"All fantasy," she clarified.

"And now?" he asked, kneeling to dry her feet.

"I'm obsessed with sex...all reality."

Carefully he dried her pubic hair, first with a towel, then with his breath. "You know what this is?" he whispered.

"A blow dry?" Smiling, she sank back onto the bed, her legs dangling onto the rug. Their lovemaking was like a gift box of chocolates. She had no idea what to expect until she was sampling it. This time he made swift and playful love to her with a darting, light-edged tongue. They ended intertwined, his head cradled on her belly. She was still wrapped in the cocoon of pleasure when the telephone rang.

Ted reached over her, fumbled for the receiver. She had a sudden memory of the second week of her marriage, lying naked, she and Mark on the precipice of excitation, he astride her when they were interrupted by the telephone. "Don't answer," she had said.

"I have to," he had insisted, "I'm on call for the hospital."

"Then hurry," she had begged. It was not the hospital but her father, and Mark had handed her the phone. She had sat naked and shivering with discomfort as she made small talk about her mother's new draperies and snow tires for the Buick. When she had hung up the phone, a ferocious fight had ensued—their first that she remembered, although Mark recalled one on their honeymoon when she had refused to make love on a midnight beach…too damp, too public, too scratchy. Strange that Mark had been the romantic one, then.

"No, of course I haven't forgotten, darling. See you at ten," Ted said, hanging up the phone. "We have a command performance this morning," he explained as he slid from the bed. He splashed cold water on his face, poked gingerly at the pouches under his eyes.

"Mother will know her prodigal son has been dissipating."

"Mother?" Julia asked.

"Surely you knew that I must have had a mother."

"No doubt. But where?"

"In the rich recesses of Russian Hill. Mother, or Mathilda, as she prefers to be called, has buried husband number three, and lives the good life with a rotating stable of beautiful young men, boring straight ones for *sex* and witty gay ones for the social ramble. And we are invited to brunch, where we put the bite on Mama."

"I can't go, Ted," Julia protested.

"Of course you can. You told Mark you'd be home today. You didn't specify a time. Stay just a little longer? Please?"

Here it was again. The plea. Stay just a little longer! And she had, and it had been exciting, exhilarating. Their evening in the city, the tennis game in the park, the conference, the night with Roger and Cass. And she was curious. She wanted to know everything about Ted that she could. What sort of mother would he have? And how would they be with each other?

Julia watched as Ted slipped into a freshly pressed white linen suit. With his gleaming auburn hair and beard he looked like a Southern plantation owner or the crown prince of Norway. Carefully, Ted tied the knot on his striped silk tie. "The only way Valanopolis will consent to my being part of the excavation again is with big money. Fifty thousand will get us the radarscope, a hundred thousand the use of a small atomic submarine. Mathilda won't even miss it. Once I can convince her to part with it, that is."

"She has that kind of money?" Julia asked.

"She has two kinds—spending and saving. I'll take either. It's not going to be easy. She swore last year that it was my last handout. Time for me to grow up and look after myself."

"Maybe she's right," Julia said, plucking a stray hair from the back of his collar.

He reached behind him, cupping her hips. "I *am* looking after myself. Come with me."

"Do you really think that's a good idea?"

"I can't do it alone," he said. "She's not going to give up without a struggle. I need you, Julia."

"You'll do fine by yourself," she assured him.

"But I want to share it with you," he said. And then he added the final persuasive touch. "And I want her to meet you."

Julia rested her head against the broad slope of his back, inhaling his scent, citrus and musk. "How long will it take?"

"No more than an hour, I promise."

She sighed. "What should I wear?"

9

The lady looked in fighting trim, Julia thought, as half
an hour later she assayed the small erect figure framed
by a massive bay window whose expansive view spanned
both bridges. Julia and Ted had been ushered into the
three-story brick town house by a uniformed maid, who
then led them up a curving mahogany staircase to the
enormous living room furnished in blue satins and vel-
vets, floral Aubusson carpets, and Directoire tables with
gleaming marble tops and the legs of *en pointe* ballerinas.
In the midst of the splendor stood Mathilda, poised and
angular in black silk, with the same blazing green eyes of
her son and the same, albeit carefully restored, red-gold
hair.

She extended her arms to Ted, and Julia could feel the
guarded warmth between them flicker like pale winter

sunlight. The two embraced formally, a kiss on each cheek, and Mathilda led the way to the dining room. The table was laid with a Belgian lace cloth, crystal bowls of papaya and pineapple nestling in crushed ice, a warmer of flaky croissants, and two silver pots. "Do you still fancy chocolate?" Mathilda asked her son. He nodded and laughed aloud as she dropped a marshmallow into the steaming cup with sugar tongs. "Some nursery tastes still prevail, I assume?" she said. "And who is your lovely friend...a flight attendant, an actress, perhaps?"

"This is Julia Simon, Mathilda. She's a professor of dramatic art in Los Angeles."

Mathilda's feathery eyebrows arched. "An academic? So was Theodore, once."

"Before I trod the primrose path of dalliance," Ted added, "strewing my mother's money like rose petals."

"A romantic mother breeds a profligate son," Mathilda said, passing the petit fours. "A Gustafson aphorism. Theodore was conceived in a gondola on the Grand Canal in Venice. I spent the next two weeks on the Amalfi Drive with his father, who was as beautiful as Michelangelo's David and about as marriageable. He ran off with the mâitre d' of our hotel in Capri. Terrible food, I remember. I came home pregnant with Theodore...my Italian souvenir."

Julia sipped her coffee, resisting an impulse to applaud politely at the no doubt familiar aria that was being performed especially for her.

"A lifelong albatross, Mathilda, dear," Ted said, smiling. "Here for another hang around your neck."

Mathilda stirred her coffee, the emeralds on her wrist and fingers fracturing the sunlight. "More money, Theodore? How mundane."

"Money always is." Ted's shrug was charming. "But this time it's not for speculation. This time I have the proof."

He drew his chair closer to his mother's and began to detail the excavation. Julia watched as Mathilda's face slowly changed, reflecting Ted's excitement. Her eyes mirroring his fire, echoing his smile; even their rapid breathing meshed. It wasn't only vicarious, a mother loving her son and by extension his projects, Julia thought; but Mathilda loved the magic itself, the possible unearthing of a marvel. Ted went on to describe the equipment he would need—the sonar, the submersible, the tethered robot. Mathilda sipped the last of her coffee, daintily spooning the melted sugar from the bottom. "How much?" she asked.

"Time? Equipment?" he asked.

"Money," she countered. "The rest doesn't concern me."

Ted looked directly at his mother, with the same intensity, Julia recalled, with which he had first looked at her on the airplane. "A quarter of a million," he said.

"Goes up every year," Mathilda said with a frown.

"Just like the cost of living," Ted said.

"The cost of dreaming," she amended. "When are you going to grow up and stop digging in the sand?"

"This is digging underwater, Mother, much more grown-up. You need a bigger shovel."

Mathilda twisted the large round emerald on her finger like the dial of a combination lock. Her green eyes beneath the heavy hooded lids met Julia's. "I shouldn't give it to him," she said softly.

Julia watched as Mathilda's gaze shifted to Ted. She thought of her own boy, Davey, standing before her with bright expectant eyes. "Can I go to the concert, Mom? Please, they're the greatest." Or "I've got to have new skis and boots. I want to race this year." Or "Can I have a dirt bike? It's not dangerous, honest, it's not." Yes, she had said, yes, to please him, to foster his daring, to support his passion.

"We'll call the dig...Situ Mathilda—how about that? You'll have your own spot in the Aegean, in the heart of a volcano," Ted offered.

Mathilda poured herself a fresh cup of coffee. "A monument of ash. Very fitting." She sipped her second cup slowly, making him wait. Then, "If I give you this money, it will be the last of your inheritance," she said finally. "There'll be nothing left."

"I'm willing to take that risk," he said.

"Are you sure?" she asked. "It's a big risk."

"Great loves and great achievements require great risks. That's a Gustafson aphorism." Ted jumped to his feet and embraced his mother's silk clad shoulders. "Thank you, darling." He paused, then said, "Okay if we meet at the bank tomorrow at ten?"

She smiled. "Take the money and run?"

"And fly," he corrected. "It's faster. You won't regret it, Mother." He knelt by the side of her chair. "You'll be helping to unearth the greatest temple of the ancient world. You'll be proving that Atlantis exists, that Utopia is real."

"If Atlantis once existed, it was not a utopia. The meaning of utopia is 'no place.'" Mathilda looked pointedly at Julia. "Will you be going?"

"Very soon, I hope," Ted answered, lacing his fingers through Julia's, pulling her to her feet. He wheeled about to blow a kiss to his mother. "See you tomorrow," he called.

"I don't doubt it," Mathilda answered dryly.

As the heavy carved front door closed behind them, Ted leaped into the air, clicking his heels in an impressive display of balletic grace. Shades of a Broadway musical, Julia thought. If you're happy, dance; if you're in love, sing. Now he was holding her hand, guiding her down the steep slope of Russian Hill. "She came through. It's going to happen. God, I'm happy. You're going to love Thera."

"Someday maybe," she said.

"When things get settled," he said. "There's a branch of the American University. You could teach." He turned toward her, peered at her sober face. "What's wrong?"

"Nothing."

"You're upset about the money." He voiced her thoughts. "A grown man shouldn't take money from his mother. It's irresponsible, unmanly?"

"Well, it *is* her money."

"For the moment. In time it will be mine. I'm borrowing it."

"But even so it's family money," she insisted. "If the project is really worthwhile shouldn't it be funded by a research foundation or a university?"

"Schliemann unearthed the walls of Troy with his own money. Evans excavated Knossos with his own money. No one will ever fund the really good stuff until after it's been proven, and then the fun's gone. Just you watch Valanopolis come round when I show him the money," he chortled.

They came to the bottom of the hill, began climbing

the next. Ted kissed her forehead. "Do I see a worry line?"

She shrugged. "You're always so sure of what you want. And you'll do whatever is necessary to get it. I see life in a welter of contingencies."

"Priorities, love. You've got to know what counts and move toward it." His arm circled her waist, and together they strode up the hill, Julia breathing hard, Ted moving with the glide of a mountaineer. She loved the hard muscles of his thighs, his smell, the sunlight glinting off his beard. He was all that was silk and chocolate in her life. If only she had met him when she was twenty, before she had made so many other choices. And yet she knew that she would not have gone with him then, would not have been brave or certain enough. Was she brave and certain enough now?

What would it be like to start all over again, knowing what she now knew, not making the same mistakes, not allowing those walls to be built, those frozen silences. Making pleasure and appreciation priorities. And never stop making love, for it was the glue that kept man and woman together.

They walked past the canopied condominiums, the rococo Nob Hill hotels, the parking garages, the august Pacific Union Club, the rose window of Grace Cathedral, until they came to a curious concrete dome. From somewhere within came the strains of koto music, the notes falling like flower petals. A smiling man in a purple kimono standing outside beckoned them in. A carved wooden sign said Watercourse Way Zen Temple. She hesitated, but Ted led the way, whispering, "We haven't given thanks yet." She followed him; it seemed a good idea to ask for guidance on this particular Sunday.

The hall was austere, its only decorations a calligraphic scroll, a small wooden table and upon it an artful arrangement of three white chrysanthemums. The service was ending. Final rhythmic chants were being softly intoned by the parishioners. Then in Japanese and in English, the Zen priest suggested that the assembled congregation use the remainder of the time for zazen, silent meditation. In the quiet of the temple, Julia's thoughts teemed.

"Beware if you follow your feelings, for they are crooked as corkscrews." Yeats's admonition rose in her memory. She rested her palms against the cool wooden railing, remembering the photos of Zen meditation gardens, craggy rocks set among raked sand, which with the shifting patterns of sun and shade the mind's eye transformed into islands amid wave-lapped seas. We see the world as we choose to see it. Two weeks ago she had wanted Michael. The dream of Michael, handsome, dashing, famous; Michael as written by Rostand, Michael as written by Shakespeare. She had imagined playing his leading lady; unfortunately, she hadn't gotten the part.

Now she had Ted, her beautiful bronze Buddha. She stole a glance at him, at his strongly etched profile, sensuous mouth. He caught her gaze and acknowledged it with a lazy wink. She wanted him right now. Wanted her arms around him, her eyes feasting on the strong symmetry of his face. He tasted so good and moved so well. His laugh released her own. He could mime and clown and sing on key; he could dance and carry her with him like a sail in the wind. He was all the prizes she had never won. And he wanted her. She needed to reach out to him before it was too late. Before she was too old.

She had not seen his like before, would not see it again. Should she dare to surrender, to dive into the alchemist's fire, to eschew the civil, the expected, the compromised? To court abandon? If not now...when? Mark would be hurt, confused, lost for a while; he loved her in his way. But he was so closed, so unavailable. And she had become the same way, only giving him the shell of herself. In time, Mark would heal. He would have his practice, their friends and single women in droves; a divorced physician was a welcome addition to any dinner party. And after his feelings of marital outrage had banked, he would remember their happier times, she hoped. As for Davey, he would be sadly disillusioned at a vulnerable time. It was a painful thought, but, she reasoned, he was already turning away from her as the polestar in his life.

But what of Wendy, Julia's freckled, gangly mirror image? She could not leave her. She would have to take Wendy with her to Greece, tear her away from her family, her language, her country, to follow her mother's lover on his quest for Atlantis. But was it not just as much her own quest? She would give her daughter that example of risk, of daring, of not needing to know the end before opening the book. Both she and Wendy would learn the richness of another culture. Kids adjusted to moves all the time—in military families, diplomatic families. But what if Wendy wouldn't go or if Mark refused to let her?

Julia's thoughts buzzed into silence as she heard an ecstatic murmuring beside her. Her attention was drawn to a heavyset woman dressed in a red silk embroidered robe, her face pale as unbaked bread upon which black eyebrows and scarlet lips had been drawn. The woman was praying rapturously, but something in her clenched knuckles and rigid back spoke less of faith than of desperation, of religion as reparation. She was reminiscent of all those women Julia had known who, in later life, became fierce devotees of Jung, or feminism, of holistic health.

Julia thought of the divorcees who dressed like their teenaged daughters in tight jeans and braless T-shirts, who smiled too broadly at college boy waiters and dutiful bartenders. She thought of the spinsters who dressed like Hopi kachina dolls in fringes and feathers or like East Indians in yards of gauze and powdered red bindis. A tremor of fear, of foreboding rose. What if Ted left her or she him, and she was set adrift, no longer the college instructor, the doctor's wife, the suburban housewife? Who would she be? How would she know herself?

The congregation rose, silently walking in single file toward the open door. Julia and Ted took their places in the line. At the threshold, framed in sunlight, stood an elderly Japanese gentleman clad in a pin-striped kimono. As each person stopped before him, he reached into a wooden barrel and, with ceremonial dignity, presented each one with a shiny red apple.

As Julia accepted her apple, felt its weight and roundness fill her palm, she whispered to Ted, "It's a symbol."

"Of what?" he asked.

"Of Zen. Of wholeness, of completeness." She paused, studying the apple. "The fruit contains the seed. The seed contains the fruit. Different in form, yet one and the same."

"So?" he said.

"So the message is to trust in growth and change. All

things rise and pass away." She stopped, flushed with pleasure at her insight. "Don't you think?"

Ted's smile was reflective, mischievous. "What if it's the apple of discord, the one that began the Trojan War? Or the apple on the tree of knowledge that led to the fall and the expulsion from Eden?"

She gazed at the shining apple as if it were a crystal ball or the entrails of a sacred dove. It became numinous, no longer an object of playful speculation, but an augury, a vehicle of divination.

Ted studied her quizzical face for a moment, then ambled back to the gentleman in the kimono. The man stood alone, the worshippers dispersed.

"We are having an ecclesiastical debate, sir. Perhaps you can help us?" Ted asked. "Can you tell us the meaning of the apple?"

The elderly gentleman met Ted's gaze politely, but seemed not to comprehend.

"The apple is clearly a religious symbol," Julia added. "But of what, exactly?"

The old man thought for a long time, then slowly, in lightly accented English, replied, "I own an orchard. At harvest time, I bring apples to share with the congregation. It is a healthy snack."

Ted chortled and tossed his apple high into the air in a graceful arabesque. "So much for symbol hunting," he said, threading his arm through hers. "You're going to have to make this decision without divine guidance, Julie-bean, all by your imperfect self."

So there was no waiting answer, no oracle, only her own troubled mind. How she longed for a sign. It's why we read fortune cookies and horoscopes, she thought. Anything for direction. Her marriage was unsatisfying and familiar; the future with Ted was tantalizing but unknown.

"Will you be coming to Greece?" he asked.

"I'm not ready to make that decision yet."

"When will you be ready?"

"I don't know," she said.

"When you go back to L.A.?"

"Maybe."

"I can go with you."

"Not a good idea," she said, and then in an effort to end the conversation, pointed toward the stairs carved into the hill. "Look, this hill is tiered like Borobudur." She selected the reference to surprise him, to charm him. In time he would grow to know all her stories, but not yet.

"Like what?" he asked.

"Borobudur in Java. It's the largest Buddhist temple in the world."

He shrugged. "I'm a classicist, babe, all I know are the Greeks."

"They built the temple so that the higher you climb, the less steep the steps become; just as when you approach enlightenment the path becomes easier. The first terraces are carved with scenes from Buddha's life, teaching tales, but as you climb, the forms grow more and more abstract, like God himself."

Ted brushed her cheek with his knuckles, "And you, my love—is your journey to enlightenment becoming easier?"

She drew closer to him. "I'm afraid I haven't left the realm of fear and desire yet."

They were nearing the crest of the hill now, a few yards from the hotel entrance. "Maybe when I get older," she began, then stopped, her breath catching in her throat. There under the canopy of the hotel stood a tall slender man with close-cropped gray hair squinting in the sunlight. "Oh, my God," she gasped.

"What's wrong?" Ted followed her gaze with questioning concern.

But how could Ted have known? Picked this man out amid dozens of others, tourists and businessmen? He was hers, part of her life.

Unsteadily, she walked the few remaining feet to the waiting man and greeted him with an awkward embrace. "Ted," she said, "this is my husband, Mark. Mark, this is Ted Gustafson." The two men eyed each other warily. Ted proffered his hand and Mark took it, although the space between them was as charged as a minefield. Julia stepped into that space gingerly and the three of them entered the darkened sanctuary of the lobby.

Julia's mind was racing. Why had Mark come? What had he found out? Suspected? Intuited? She had been discreet, circumspect. Yet on some deep level his appearance was not a surprise. It felt necessary, even inevitable. Julia waited for Ted to leave, to excuse himself, but he made no move to do so. Perhaps this was the omen, she thought. The propitious time. The moment of truth.

She seized the initiative. "There's a coffee shop on the lower level," she said, and led the way. In the elevator, she stood between the two men, her throat dry, breath shallow, knees trembling, the same type of backstage jitters she had felt before a performance, a high adrenaline mixture of fear and excitement. But it felt right that this was happening, almost a relief. She had kept the two men juxtaposed in her mind; it was appropriate that they meet. The rehearsal period was over. It was time to play the scene.

Mark had dressed carefully, Julia noted, in his navy serge suit, his wedding and funeral suit, slightly out of style now with its too-broad lapels. She had mended the jacket lining just before she left. There was a light dusting of dandruff on his shoulder. Reflexively, her hand rose to brush it away, then stopped.

They entered the café and a waitress, in striped pinafore and cap, showed them to a table and handed them three shiny pink menus. When the waitress reappeared with her pad and pencil, Julia, although her stomach was stone heavy, dutifully ordered the Nob Hill Special, a Monte Cristo sandwich. Both men ordered only coffee. Chagrined, she had a vision of herself cutting and chewing a deep fried morass while they ascetically, judiciously sipped their coffee and decided her fate. It was her Jewish childhood coming up to haunt her; when all else fails, eat.

Their waitress poured three brimming cups of coffee. "Does anyone take cream?" the woman asked. Again, only Julia did. She added the cream to her coffee, then held the steaming cup in her hands for warmth and comfort. She raised her eyes, not quite meeting Mark's waiting gaze, and broke the silence. "How did you find me?" she asked.

"I saw Harry Sokolov at the hospital," Mark said.

"Oh?"

"He said that they'd seen you in San Francisco."

"That's right. On the tennis courts," she said.

"I told Harry I was trying to reach you. Luckily, he remembered the name of your friend," Mark continued, "and the conference hotel. I called a number of times and left messages, but you were out. So I drove up."

The waitress brought Julia's Nob Hill Special. The rich aroma of the batter fried bread made her stomach lurch. She pushed the plate away, fighting a rising wave of nausea. Beneath the screen of the table, she felt Ted take her hand. She let her fingers rest in his for a moment, then eased it away. Not in front of Mark…not yet.

"You didn't have to come," she said. "I was flying back today."

"I know," Mark said. "But I had something important to tell you."

The gravity of his voice startled her. "Something to tell you." Mark's appearance was not what she thought at all. It was worse. Far worse. Terrifying images flashed before her eyes. A car crash. Davey, his slender neck broken; Wendy, her life blood spilling onto a highway. Retribution for Julia's sins.

"What?" she gasped.

Mark looked pointedly at Ted. Did she want this stranger to hear?

"It's all right," she said. She couldn't bear the tension a minute longer. "Please tell me."

"It's your mother," Mark said softly.

"What?"

"She's suffered a relapse," he said. "The cancer's spread. It's in her lungs, in her bone marrow. She's in the hospital."

"How bad is it?"

Mark studied the ground as if it threatened to open. "Very bad...she's dying."

His words were like a blow from behind. She clutched the rim of the table. For a moment it was all that kept her from spinning off into space. "What hospital is she in?"

"Mount Sinai."

"Did you talk to my dad?"

"Yes, he's doing all right. He's a strong man."

She nodded. "I've got to go see them."

"Do you want me to come with you?" Mark asked.

"No," she said, moved by his offer. "I think it's better if I go alone. Will you tell the children I'll be back in a few days?"

"You can tell them yourself."

"What do you mean?" She had a sudden vision of Mark whisking off the tablecloth to reveal the children crouching beneath.

"They're upstairs in the lobby. I had no one to leave them with," he explained.

As if on cue, the waitress brought the check and placed it face down at Mark's saucer. Of course, Julia thought, he was the oldest, the most dignified, the power figure. Ted nodded his thanks as Mark paid the check.

As the three of them entered the lobby, she wondered how to introduce Ted to the children. She could neither include nor dismiss him. But she needn't have worried. To the children, he was virtually invisible. They sat sprawled upon a red velvet sofa, Davey listlessly twisting Wendy's wrist as she pretended to struggle and pull away toward freedom. Davey looked up and, seeing them, released Wendy, who flew to Julia, flinging her scrawny arms around her mother's hips.

Julia hugged the spare little body close. The child's weight was almost fluid, pouring into her center like milk in a bowl. She pushed her daughter's dark hair back from her forehead. Her bangs were clumped with sweat; she needed a bath and the hem of her denim skirt was unraveling.

"How are you, sweetheart? How was camp? Did you have fun?" The automatic chatter of parenthood. Not waiting for the child's answer, she moved toward Davey, who averted his cheek from her kiss of greeting. "How's it going?" she asked. "Dad tells me you won all the trophies." The boy mumbled something unintelligible and slumped into a chair in the farthest corner.

Just in the past three weeks it seemed he had grown taller, broader in the chest and shoulders. Julia was suddenly conscious of the tangles of golden hair on his forearms, the peach fuzz downing his chin and upper lip, the curving, humorous mouth now freed of its twisted metal braces. He would be a striking young man. And Wendy, water sprite, still looking like *Mad* magazine's logo, with her coffee-bean eyes and jack-o'-lantern grin, already possessed an incipient dancer's torso, a snake charmer's grace. Julia held the little girl at arm's length. "Did Dad tell you that I have to go to New York?"

"But you just came back from Greece," the child protested.

"I know, but Grandma's very sick. I have to go and see her."

"Then I'm going with you," she said.

"You can't, sweetie."

"Why not? There's no school, just day camp. I hate day camp. They make you pass all those stupid tests."

"What kind of tests?" she asked absently.

"Swimming," the child said.

"But you're a good swimmer," she said.

"I don't care." Wendy lifted her face, bright and searing as a torch. "I want to be with you."

"It'll be sad," Julia cautioned.

"I know." Wendy slipped her hand into Julia's. The covenant was sealed. That much was settled; she was going. She flashed a quick look of triumph at her brother, but his gaze was inward, his mouth drawn tight like their father's.

"Okay, I'm going upstairs to pack. You stay here," Julia

said firmly. Reluctantly, Wendy resumed her place on the velvet sofa.

"I'll be down in ten minutes," Julia said, and headed for the elevator. As she passed Ted, she caught his eye in a mute appeal for patience. She hurried to her room, crammed her remaining clothes into a suitcase, then called the airline, booking two seats to New York. A call to her parents' apartment went unanswered. Then she phoned her aunt Belle, her mother's older sister. Her aunt's quavering voice sobbed in her ear. "Why such suffering? She was a good person. How can God permit it?"

As she heard Ted's key, Julia cut through her aunt's lament. "Belle, tell Dad I'm flying in tonight with Wendy. I'll meet him at the apartment. I'll see you at the hospital tomorrow."

Ted stood framed in the doorway. As she hung up the phone, he walked quickly toward her, taking her in his arms. For a moment she let herself yield, lean against him as he kneaded the tight muscles in her neck and shoulders, but as his hands moved lower, running softly across her back, she pulled away, alarmed by the rising rivulet of desire.

An unbidden memory. She was thirteen, riding back from the cemetery after her grandmother's funeral with her cousin Robert, a month older, sitting next to her in the crowded back seat, thighs touching, his forearm brushing her newly budding breast. The two of them flushed and sweaty in the flower scented black limousine. Eros and Thanatos, never far apart.

Julia slammed shut the lid of her suitcase, tugged at the locks. A live sponge that she had brought back from Greece for her mother was blocking the closure. Ted reached in and pressed it down.

"How long will you be gone?" he asked.

"I don't know."

"I'll meet you wherever you say. New York, Los Angeles, Greece."

She was silent. "Live," her mother had said. "Live, Julia. I never did."

"Mark looks different than I expected," Ted mused.

"What do you mean?"

He shrugged, searching for words. "I don't know. He just seems like a nice guy."

She nodded. "He is."

"I'll miss you," Ted said.

She touched her hand to his cheek, gingerly, like testing a heating skillet. "I'll call you," she said, then, lifting her suitcase, left the room.

Mercifully, the ride to the airport was short. Julia sat in the back with Wendy, Davey up front with Mark. Davey turned on the baseball game, and the familiar litany of balls and strikes filled the silence of the car, speaking of lazy Sunday afternoons. When they arrived at the terminal, Davey made no move to leave the car. Julia leaned over the front seat. "Do you want to come to New York with me?" she asked.

He shook his head, his mouth slack with simulated disinterest. "What for? It sounds depressing."

"I just want you to know that you can if you choose to."

"Well, I don't," he said flatly. "And anyway, I can't afford to miss practice." His eyes never left the radio, as if he could see beyond it to the cheering stands, the figures rounding home, the changing scoreboard.

"Then you'll stay with Dad, and I'll see you in a few days. I'll talk to you before," she said, touching his knee.

"Whatever." He permitted the touch but did not return it. He had sensed something amiss, Julia thought, and was dealing with that knowledge in the typical male way of emotional distancing.

Julia waited as Mark removed their suitcases from the trunk. Anticipating the likelihood of Wendy's decision to accompany Julia to New York, he had packed some clothes for her.

Wendy hugged her father hard. "I wish you were coming, Daddy."

"Me, too, darling," he said, lifting her high in his arms. Julie watched through the beginning of tears. So much disruption, so many goodbyes. Why was she adding to it?

As they boarded the plane, the flight attendant provided Wendy with a packet of diversions: crayons, coloring book, puzzles, pilot's wings and a coveted deck of playing cards. At Wendy's cajoling, Julia absently played game after game of casino, go fish and rummy while Wendy carefully toted up the score on an air sickness bag. In between games, Wendy became acquainted with their neighbors on both sides, made numerous trips to the bathroom, caught her finger in the seat-belt clasp, and cadged a special vegetarian lunch. She finally fell asleep, wrapped in two blankets, propped up on three pillows.

Julia sat, cradling a glass of red wine, her eyes dully fixed on the moving shadows of the screen, Wendy's body like an anchor across her lap. She stroked the child's silky black hair, listened to her noisy rhythmic breathing.

"Astride of a grave and a difficult birth. Down in the hole, lingeringly, the gravedigger puts on the forceps." Beckett again. Birth and death joined in one fleeting poetic image. The image spoke to her, helping to give shape and coherence to the last few days; the flowering of her own body as her mother's edged toward death.

Better not to think about it, just act. She drew her daughter's small form closer to her breast, grateful for its insistent weight.

10

Julia scanned the waiting crowd at the gate for her father, but it was Wendy who spotted him first. She freed herself from her mother's hand and ran hurtling against her grandfather's legs. Her arms encircled his waist. "You've grown a big belly, Papa."

"A big candy belly," he said, hugging her. He handed her an oversize chocolate bar. "Now you can grow one, too."

Julia turned to her father. They embraced quickly, decorously; tears, much too close, were useless now, an indulgence.

"Aren't you surprised to see me, Grandpa?" Wendy demanded.

"Yes, darling, but I'm glad you came."

"Me, too," she said, tucking her hand in his. "Did you bring your red car?"

"Yes, I did," he said.

"Is Grandma in the car?"

"No, darling, Grandma's in the hospital."

"Oh, yeah, I forgot," she said quickly, stuffing her mouth with chocolate.

"You can see her tomorrow," her grandfather said. "If you want to?"

"Sure I do," she said fuzzily, chocolate coating her tongue. "I'm not afraid."

They entered the car. "I know you're not," her grandfather said, cupping her knee. "You're a big girl."

The familiar gesture of assurance; Julia could feel her father's hand on her own eight-year-old knee as a tooth was being pulled or a splinter removed, as a roller coaster eased its way up the vertical slope, before a spelling bee began or a camp bus departed. Her father's hands, those broad knuckles dusted with black wiry hairs, the white half-moon nails. She leaned over and lightly covered his hand with her own.

Once back at the apartment, she and Wendy bedded down in the spare room. Wendy fell asleep quickly and slept soundly, while Julia's sleep was fitful, although mercifully dreamless. The next morning, although the radio predicted rain, sunshine streamed through the window. It was only eight, but Julia's father was out, observing a New York ritual—moving his car to the alternate side of the street to avoid a ticket. He had left coffee brewing for her, and packaged cereal for Wendy.

The ride to the hospital was mostly silent, with occasional observations about traffic, potholes, the rising humidity. They drove around the hospital several times until they were able to find a parking spot four long blocks away. So many people were involved in the tall white building, Julia thought, as they walked through the revolving door, past the uniformed guard, the information desk. The gift shop with its flowers, bed jackets and romance novels. The cafeteria, the newsstand. The rubber-soled, white-clad nurses, the ambulatory patients in blue cotton robes and backless slippers.

Julia had been a hospital patient only twice, and each time had been rewarded with a healthy, newborn baby. Yet even so, the sight of those white plastic name bracelets, the rubber tubing, the syringes, the fluted pill cups sent a shiver down her spine.

They rode in an elevator to the eleventh floor, walked through two sets of double doors and down a long corridor to the nurse's station. A freckled-faced nurse with an Irish brogue informed them that Wendy must wait in the visitor's lounge as no one under eighteen could enter. The woman showed them to a small anteroom where two white-haired women sat, legs spread wide for balance, watching a frenzied television game show.

Wendy shyly took a seat farthest away from the women, averting her glance.

"Come sit here, honey," one of them called, resting her coffee mug on the floor. "We'll put on cartoons."

"That's all right," Wendy said softly. "I like this show better."

"Well, then, come closer where you can see it." The woman indicated a place beside her. When Wendy slipped into it, the woman patted her on the shoulder. "Don't want to strain those pretty peepers."

"Pee-pers?" Wendy giggled.

"It means eyes," Julia explained.

But Wendy had already turned her attention to the screen, shouting with the studio audience, "Number three...door number three."

Julia and her father headed down the corridor and into her mother's room. There were two beds; on the one closer to the door, a wizened, defiantly blond woman sat, her leg in a cast, talking animatedly on the phone. "Of course I don't expect him to come. Does a leopard change his spots?" She paused to cast a somber, commiserating glance in their direction, and then returned to the phone.

Julia's father pulled aside a corner of the green curtains shrouding the other bed. Despite the fact that she had steeled herself, Julia's hand flew to her mouth, stifling a cry. Her mother lay upon her back, diminished, pale, mouth slack, eyes closed.

"She's just asleep." Her father moistened a cotton ball and gently bathed his wife's forehead and parched lips. "Wake up, Bea," he whispered. "It's morning. Julia's here all the way from California. Open your eyes, darling. Say hello to your daughter." He prodded Julia's arm. "Go closer, tell her you're here."

Julia approached the side of the bed, reached over the guardrail to touch her mother's shoulder. "Mom, it's me." She watched as her mother's eyelids fluttered and with great effort opened. A flicker of blue and they shut again. Julia pushed down the rail, sat on the edge of the bed. "Are you tired, Mom?" she whispered. "Do you want to sleep?"

"Thirsty," her mother said, her voice a husky rumble.

"It's the oxygen," her father explained. He held a cup of water and a straw to his wife's mouth. "Drink, Bea," he urged, one hand beneath her head. "Just a sip." Julia watched as her mother pursed her lips around the straw, tried to draw in the fluid, but hadn't the strength. The straw fell back, spraying water onto her nightgown. "It's all right," her father said, "we'll get you a fresh one." He handed Julia a cup of ice chips. "Feed her some of these. I'll get the nurse."

Tentatively, Julia placed a sliver of ice upon her mother's tongue and waited for it to melt.

Her father returned with the nurse, a smiling, buxom, dark-skinned girl. "All right, now, Mrs. G.," she said cheerfully, "we'll have you nice and dry in two shakes. Then you can visit with your company. Your daughter favors your husband, I think, though she does have your smile. Such a handsome family you've got."

Julia watched as the young nurse deftly changed the wet gown, her mother limp as a rag doll or an infant. Julia remembered changing her own babies, poking their legs into tiny pants, thrusting a dimpled arm into a waiting sleeve. She watched as the nurse turned her mother over, revealing Bea's bruised and pitted buttocks.

Her father followed her glance. "It's the injections," he said, "the drugs, the tests. They've run out of veins."

The nurse smoothed the sheets and blankets, fluffed the pillows. She removed the untouched breakfast tray. "Can I get you folks some coffee?"

"No thanks," her father said, then added, "but it's very nice of you to ask. You're a good person, Gloria."

"Thanks, Mr. G., I'll tell my sugar that."

"Tell him he's lucky to have you. We all are." He paused. "Gloria, did you know that my little granddaughter's outside, all the way from California? She wants to see her grandmother."

"How old is she, Mr. G.?"

"She's big for her age."

"Now you know as well as I do that we can't let children in. They might infect the patients. But," she said with a smile, "if we draw the curtain, who'll be the wiser? Just for a minute, though."

A moment later she led Wendy into the room. The child tiptoed rapidly to the side of the bed, pressed up against the guardrail and stood silently watching her grandmother. It was only when Julia saw her daughter's thin chest rise and fall in synchronicity with her mother's that she realized that she, too, was mirroring her mother's breathing, the long tortuous inhalation, the rapid explosive out breath. So much effort to obtain so little air.

The only sounds in the room were those of their joint breathing, like reeds rustling in the wind. Lulled by the heat of the room, the hypnotic breathing, Julia was startled when she heard a barely audible voice and saw her mother reach out, her fingers tracing the line of Wendy's cheek and chin before falling back onto the sheet.

"What did she say, Mommy? I couldn't hear it."

"*Katzele,*" Julia answered.

"What's that?"

"It's a Yiddish word," she said, reaching into the past. "It means little kitten."

Gloria arrived to remove Wendy, who although protesting, assented. She lingered by the door. "Come keep me company, Grandpa. Please."

Unable to refuse his granddaughter's plea, Julia's father left for the lounge, while Julia kept vigil. Her mother slept, spent from the contact. Skimming the newspaper, Julia half dozed until Gloria arrived with a lunch tray. Firmly the nurse prodded her patient's shoulder. "Time for lunch, Mrs. G. We've got some nice pea soup and cherry Jell-O. Can you sit up and take a bit?"

When Julia's mother gave no response, the nurse dug out her blood pressure cuff and stethoscope, took measurements and noted them in the chart. She shook her head sadly at Julia and said, "The doctor will be in soon."

After the nurse left, Julia straightened the items on the bedside table—the flowers, the cards, the magazines. She opened the lid of a jar of lotion. Lilac. There was a lilac bush she had passed every day on her way to grade school. In the spring the scent was heady. Once, she had broken off a large branch of the purple blossoms and brought them home to her mother. Bea had admonished her for taking something that didn't belong to her, but had kept the branch in water until the final blossoms died and fell to the floor.

Julia dabbed some of the pink lotion onto her palms, finding its silky coolness comforting. "Mom, how about a back rub?" she asked. "It might feel good." Never had she offered such a service, for they were not a touching family. She studied her mother's face for an answer;

Bea's eyes were closed, but there was a flicker of response about the mouth, fleeting as a shadow. Carefully, Julia turned her mother on her side, supported her with pillows and untied the strings of the hospital gown. Warming the lotion in her hands, she slowly began to stroke her mother's back. Her skin was soft and white, unmarred and whole, and as Julia's hands moved lightly over Bea's neck and shoulders, she spoke her memories, thanking her for all the favors given—for ironed blouses and homework help, for chocolate pudding and hot lunches, for tears cried into her mother's apron at ruinous haircuts and erupted skin and social slights. Julia lost track of time, stroking her mother's pale skin, not certain if she was being heard.

Her mother spoke only once, when Julia talked of Wendy. "Does she know I'm dying?" Bea asked.

"She knows you are very sick," Julia answered.

She was refastening the strings of her mother's gown when she heard footsteps, and turned to see her father and the doctor approach. She was introduced to Dr. Rodriquez, a slender, elegantly dressed man, the soft tweeds of his jacket complementing his athletic tan. As Julia accepted the cool handclasp, met the steady gaze behind the scholarly horn-rimmed glasses, she felt a wave of relief. It was a comfort knowing that this competent, well-trained physician would take charge. He would evaluate, advise, prescribe. She remembered how grateful she had always been for Mark's medical assurance, how proud she had been of his profession. How useful and honorable a calling to help people in a time of suffering.

The doctor asked them to step outside while he conducted his examination. When he emerged, Julia was sitting on a hall gurney, her father leaning against the wall beside her. They both stood erect as he approached. Obligatory small talk first. Dr. Rodriquez had done his internship at San Francisco General and reminisced about the city, the cable cars, the summer fog. Then he looked at her with a surprisingly direct gaze. His eyes were green, like Ted's. For a moment Julia was back with her lover—inappropriate yet insistent. In the presence of death, the life force rebelled. Caught in the welter of mixed messages, she missed the doctor's first sentence.

"…it can be anytime now. We'll try to keep her comfortable." Then, glancing at her father, he continued, "We'll do what you've both asked for, Mr. Green, no heroic measures. Let nature take its course."

"When?" Julia asked.

"It's hard to say."

"A month?" She persisted, "A week?" She wanted to be there. But how long could she stay?

The doctor shook his head. "Today…tomorrow."

"No," Julia cried, her heart clenching as if she had willed this suddenness.

"It's all right," her father said quietly. "She's suffered long enough."

Julia studied her father's face. There is a time, she thought, when the body is too much a burden, too little a home.

"Thank you, Doctor," he said, "you've been a great help."

Dr. Rodriquez removed his glasses, rubbed the bridge of his nose. "I only wish we could do more. I'll be in my office this afternoon if you want to reach me. If not, I'll come by tomorrow morning."

Although neither of them had any appetite, Julia and her father decided to eat in shifts. Since Wendy insisted upon her grandfather's company, Julia remained upstairs while the two of them sought out the hospital cafeteria. She sat by her mother's bedside, letting her thoughts drift, mentally outlining her future, weighing the facts of existence with Mark against an imagined life with Ted in the same orderly way in which she had always balanced the knowns and unknowns of her life decisions. Amid the heavy balance of history, duty and safety came the remembered silken pull of Ted's mouth at her throat, at her breast, and she was awash in feelings so deep that she only dimly sensed the change in the room.

Her mother's breathing had altered, the long irregular rhythm had stilled. Had her mother stopped breathing? Julia listened hard, as if to footsteps of an intruder in the night. Nothing. Silence. Just her imagination. Then it came...the rasping gurgle, like water hurtling down a rusty drain, like a drowning. The vibration of the last departing breath as it fled the universe, mirror image to the baby's first cry of entry. Her mother had ushered in Julia's first breath as she herself had ushered in Wendy's, housing their infants until that passage into bright light and unbounded space.

Julia rose unsteadily from the chair and walked out into the corridor. She saw her father playing cat's cradle with Wendy, carefully transferring a string web from his own outstretched fingers to hers. He turned to Julia, gleaning her message, yet waiting for the words. No words came. Only a stammer, a broken wail. Gloria came running around the corner, her rubber soles squeaking on the linoleum as she rushed into Bea's room. She emerged a few minutes later, embraced Julia, Wendy, Sid in rapid sequence, her cheeks streaming with tears.

Through the blurring of disbelief and spreading grief, Julia felt sympathy for the young nurse, for she had not yet built her armor of objectivity; she was still accessible, participatory. And for her, death would be, by necessity, a frequent visitor.

They waited outside, the three of them, three generations, while the parade of professionals confirmed and made official the family death. The head nurse, then the intern, who stared in discomfort at the wall behind them as he talked, finally Dr. Rodriguez, who offered soft words of sympathy, then stood and shared their sorrow for a few moments.

Her father signed the hospital record. In a small flowered case, Gloria packed Bea's things, including the lace nightgown, still unworn, that Julia had sent as a birthday present last month. The nurse whispered something in her father's ear, to which he nodded. She returned from the hospital bed with a clear plastic sack; in the bottom dangled her mother's wedding ring. "She wanted you to have it," her father said. "Maybe someday for Wendy."

The gold band with its two small diamonds caught the light as Julia slipped it into her purse. It had always been on her mother's finger, a circle of certainty adorning her busy hands. Once, she had watched that ring emerge from the bowels of a chicken as her mother's hand plucked out two gleaming yellow globes. "Unborn eggs, filled with protein and good luck," her mother had explained. "Watch," she had said, and, popping one of the slippery golden eggs into her mouth, had swallowed it whole. Julia had watched the feat with a mixture of awe and revulsion. Years later she had read of the ancient Egyptian goddess Nut, who was said to swallow the sun each night, pass it through her body and each morning give birth to it again.

Julia and Wendy returned to her mother's room for a last moment. Bea seemed to lie in a deep, dreamless sleep like an exhausted child. Julia curled her fingers around her mother's hand, stroked her smooth forehead; all the sorrow and pain had not lined her clear white skin. Wendy peered intently at her grandmother's body, a stern, wary detective searching for hidden clues.

Julia's father joined them, eyes swollen and red. "Goodbye, darling," he said. He then kissed his wife tenderly on her lips as he had done every morning and every night for forty-three years.

As they left, they passed the attendants waiting quietly in the corridor to remove the body. Down the long hall, past the slowly walking patients trailing their IV poles, into the elevator with visitors impatiently jangling their car keys, then into the crush of the lobby. People scurried about, shedding water from raincoats and umbrellas. The predicted rain had arrived. Julia peered out through the revolving door to see a downpour, a torrent. The summer skies had opened with the force of a displaced tropical storm, pelting the concrete as if to melt it to sand again.

"I'll go get the car," her father said. "You two stay here."

"No," she insisted, "we'll all go."

They could no more be separated now than they could wait for the rain to abate. They walked the four long blocks to the car unhurriedly, letting the storm plaster their hair to their skulls, their clothing to their bodies, fill their shoes in rushing rivulets.

The phone was ringing as they entered the apartment, a long echoing wail, plaintive as an unattended child. Better than silence, Julia thought. Better to enter the darkened, airless room with some possibility of greeting.

It was her aunt. "Julia," Belle whispered, "how is she?" Before she could answer, she heard her aunt's cry, "I knew it. An hour ago. I felt such a pain in my heart like I couldn't breathe, like I was choking. Oh my God… Bea…my baby sister. I used to dress her, take her to school." She heaved a shuddering sigh. "I'll call the rest of the family, and the Bernsteins and the Taybacks. When is the funeral?"

Julia called her father to the phone, and as she ran the shower water, heard him ask quietly, "So how are you, Belle? How's your back?"

She and Wendy shucked their wet clothes on the tile floor and stepped beneath the spray. They stood silently, sharing the space, letting the hot water wash over them.

Wendy's leather sandals had bled, dying her feet red; Julia knelt and scrubbed her daughter's toes to a dull pink. When she stood, the little girl wrapped her arms around her mother's waist, held her closely, fitting her fingers along the silver striations that ribboned Julia's hips, marking the time her mother's skin had stretched to enfold her.

They rested, and by noon, when the rain had stopped, drove to the funeral home. A neon sign announcing Montefiore Memorial Chapel blazed atop a brick-and-concrete dome. Her father explained that the funeral service and burial plot were provided, at least in part, by a benevolent organization he had joined thirty years ago, the Knights of Pythias. Strange heraldic name for a club founded in the Bronx, she thought. They were ushered into a wood paneled, heavily carpeted, discreetly lit office, the chairs so thickly cushioned and thronelike that Wendy's feet dangled a full foot above the ground. The funeral director entered, greeted them with hushed sympathies, then got down to business.

First, the wording of the obituary in the *New York Times*, the language preordained: beloved wife, devoted mother, cherished grandmother, the Hebrew name of the deceased, the names of the bereaved, the location of the cemetery plot. Did Mr. Green wish to purchase a double plot so that he and his wife might share their final resting place?

"We already have a double plot," Sid Green said.

"It's good that you'll be together," Julia offered.

"But when you visit, don't forget to call first," her father said.

The director looked from one to the other, saw the thread of play, relaxed his shoulders, grateful for the small touch of lightness. He continued. Did Mr. Green want eternal care for the plot? Yearly Yahrtzeit services? What sort of flowers? Grave cover? Memorial stone? How many limousines? Did he have his own rabbi or should the chapel provide one? Should the coffin lid be open or closed?

Julia's thoughts drifted back to rituals past—her wedding, where her mother had sat, anxious and confused, as Mark's mother, far more affluent and socially confident, made extravagant decisions about food, drink and decoration. Years later, Davey's bar mitzvah, she and Mark had argued about it, Mark wanting an eclectic new spun rite of passage, and she, surprising herself, clinging to the traditional forms, the synagogue, the Talmudic selections, the twisted Sabbath bread.

What new rituals awaited her? she wondered. How does one honor the undoing of a marriage? The dismantling of a home? The unraveling of a family?

The men had stopped talking, were on their feet; she felt Wendy's warm hand in hers. Julia relinquished the small suitcase she had brought to an attendant. It contained Bea's sky-blue silk dress and the matching shoes she had worn only once because they blistered her heels.

They entered the elevator, a spacious golden cage, and descended three floors below. The casket chamber was a vast labyrinth, room upon room filled with elevated carpeted platforms, and on each one rested an open coffin. Discreet white placards listed the salient features of each: wood, metal or fiberglass, its name, its lining, its range of color. Only price was omitted; that would be supplied upon request.

The funeral director gestured toward a plain wooden coffin. "This is the casket that is included in your policy. A sturdy traditional model. Perfectly adequate."

Sid Green ran his palm over the knotty pine finish. "What else would you suggest?" he asked.

The director gestured to a metallic gray coffin. Julia shuddered. "No, it looks like a bank vault."

The director paused, then, pirouetting, touched a richly gleaming mahogany box. "This is our most popular model."

Wendy insisted upon being picked up so she could see the tufted white satin lining. "That's pretty," she whispered. "Do you think Grandma will like it?"

The director cast Julia a look of discomfort; death, like sex, like divorce was hard to simplify for children.

"I think she will," Sid said, pointing to the mahogany coffin. "We'll take that one."

"That model is a thousand dollars more," the director said.

Her father did not comment on the statement until long moments afterward, as they sat in the car. "That's what it would have cost us to fly to California to visit you. Your mother was worried about the money. So who's to worry now?" He eased the car along the buckled and broken pavement of the Grand Concourse. "Live while you can, Julia. We can never know about tomorrow."

So now the advice had come from both her parents. For the first time that day, her thoughts turned to Ted.

When they arrived back at the apartment, Julia made the family's favorite quick dinner, scrambled eggs and toast. She made it just the way her mother had, adding cream cheese to the beaten eggs and grilling the toast with a sugar-cinnamon coating. Afterward, Wendy and Sid curled up on the couch, with a bowl of black licorice for dessert, Wendy laughing with surprised pleasure that her favorite sitcom had found its way across the country. Julia stood at her mother's sink, sponging the familiar white plates, their gold borders worn thin by long use. Those plates had endured from her childhood. And food would continue to be served upon them, eaten or pushed aside, and the plate would once again be washed, dried and stacked away.

"Have you called Mark?" her father asked.

"Not yet," she said. "I'll phone him tonight, then I can speak to Davey, too. Do you want me to call anyone for you?"

Her father lit a fresh cigarette, turned it around between his fingers. "Your mother was always after me to quit smoking. She was afraid I was going to get lung cancer. She never smoked, ate all the right foods. So what good did it do?" He inhaled deeply, then stubbed out the cigarette. "No, you don't have to call anyone. Belle will tell everyone. Then they'll call us."

As if on cue, her cell phone rang. She picked it up on the first ring, heard her name spoken, the connection as strong and close as an embrace. "I hope this isn't a bad time. I wanted to find out about your mother," Ted said. "How is she?"

"She's…" Her lips stumbled on the next word. Confused, she wanted to say "dead," but instead used her father's term, "passed away." But she couldn't continue speaking to Ted in his presence.

"Hold on," she said. "I'm going to take this in another room." She avoided her father's gaze, yet still felt compelled to offer an excuse. "It's quieter in the bedroom." A sudden memory of dancing with her father at her wedding. Sid, uncharacteristically a bit drunk, confiding, "Imagine, my little girl, sleeping with a man."

She sat upon the edge of her bed, her legs curled under her. "I'm here," she said.

"Julia, I'm so sorry. Did you get there in time?"

"Yes," she said, "just."

"That's good. That was important. How's your father doing?"

"Hanging on. He's strong."

"And you?"

"Dazed, I think. I don't really believe it yet."

"Big changes take time. You've had quite a few."

"Look, Ted, about us, I don't know if I can—" she began.

"Don't think about it now," he said. "Let's get through this first. When is the funeral?"

"Thursday morning."

"I miss you, Julia."

"I miss you, too." She drew the phone closer to her cheek as if it were his hand. "So much has happened," she sighed.

"You don't have to make any decisions yet. One day at a time."

A long silence followed, where she groped for an appropriate closing. Finally, she murmured, "Thanks for calling."

She could almost see him smile at the formality. "Thanks for answering," he said. Then softly, just before severing the connection, he added, "I love you."

Her response was a quick involuntary intake of breath. But no reciprocal words.

She stood staring at a pink satin pillow bought to preserve her mother's careful hairdo, thinking of the times she had spoken those dutiful words of love to Mark for peace, for kindness, for appearances. And sometimes, long ago, for real.

"Was that Daddy?" Wendy asked, her voice shrill with suspicion.

"No," Julia said, "it was a friend of Mommy's."

"Who?" the little girl demanded.

"That man you met at the hotel on Sunday, Mr. Gustafson."

"The one with the red beard," she said, scrunching up her face. "He was weird looking."

"Why do you say that?"

"I don't know," she said, moving closer. "He just was. Don't you think so?"

Once, there had been a male colleague at the university with whom she had collaborated on a theater piece. Each time he came to the house for a working session

Davey would plant himself in the living room and, if he could, squeeze his chair between theirs. That same self-protective instinct seemed operant in Wendy now.

"When is Daddy going to call?" she asked.

"I don't know," Julia said. "Do you want to call him?"

"Yes." The little girl raced eagerly to the phone. "Don't tell me," she shouted, "I know how to dial it myself. First a 1 then 213." She sat up straight, her face serious, composed. Her voice was loud and distinct. "Davey, this is Wendy. May I talk to Dad please? No, I can't tell you. I have to tell Dad first.... Dad, this is Wendy. I have to tell you some bad news." There was a breathy pause, then, "Grandma died. I saw her in the hospital and we went to the coffin place and I'm going to the funeral. How are you?"

She listened for a while, then passed the phone to Julia. "He wants to talk to you first, then to Grandpa." The conversation was hushed and earnest. The particulars were given, the cause of death, the details of the burial arrangements.

"Davey and I can take the red-eye in on Wednesday," Mark said.

"Won't that be difficult?" she demurred. "What about your patients?"

She visualized Mark, dark suited, stern visaged, standing beside her, at the rabbi's speech, the grave site, during the condolence calls. Mark was discomforted by public emotion, religious ceremony and like most physicians had yet to combat his own fear of death.

"I can cancel my appointments. Your folks' apartment is small. We'll stay at the Edison," he continued. "That should work out?"

"That's fine," she said. It was good that he was coming. Good for the family. For appearances. A seeming example of solidity, of love, of endurance. Even if it was only a brave front.

"How are you doing?" he asked. "Are you feeling better?"

"About what?"

"Everything."

"Everything?" she repeated, answering a question with a question, an old Talmudic trick.

"I want you to come home, Julia. I want things back to normal."

She sighed, as if releasing the counterpart of the breath she had taken in with Ted. "I'll see you on Thursday," she said. Then she added softly, "It's good that you're coming."

11

The day of the funeral began with the radio's weather forecast of gathering clouds, rain likely by midmorning. Neither Julia nor Wendy had brought raincoats. Sid went next door to borrow one for Wendy, an oversize yellow slicker, which she was too diffident to refuse but wily enough to forget. For Julia he offered her mother's, a suitably somber navy blue. She neither refused nor forgot it, although it was too wide for her body, too short for her legs. She wore it like a penance.

The limousine was waiting as they left the building. The amenities of tragedy, Julia thought—ambulances, squad cars, hearses. Misfortune bestowed privilege; it would be unseemly to drive oneself. The limo driver stopped at the midtown hotel to pick up Mark and Davey, who had arrived the night before. Her father greeted them with a warm embrace and an apology that the apartment was too small to house them all.

"It's okay, Sid. I understand," Mark said.

"You're a family," Sid insisted. "You should all be together." Then he added, "It means a lot to me that you're here."

When they arrived at the funeral chapel it was filled with people, the men in satin skullcaps, the women in black veils, sober visaged, teary. Julia was greeted with moist handclasps, embraces and lipstick smeared kisses as distant cousins whispered their names; some she had not seen since her wedding. Her mother's sisters wept openly, Belle dabbing at the black streams of mascara that trickled to the corners of her mouth, Cynthia's shoulders heaving with sobs. Her cousin Robert arrived, grown portly and gray. Did he remember, Julia wondered, that long-ago limo ride?

Mark was greeted with great respect for his medical credentials. In Jewish circles, doctors were highly esteemed. Davey was said to be "quite the young man" and asked if he, too, was going to be a doctor. There were clucks of admiration for Wendy, sighs of recognition at how she resembled Julia at that age, the same coloring, the same lanky frame. The child endured the embraces of her aged relatives as they reached out with arthritic hands to stroke her hair or cheek in the same way they would lean forward to touch the gleaming Torah on the high holy days as it was carried through the aisles of the synagogue, a magical symbol of rebirth and renewal.

At the funeral director's signal, Julia and her family were led into the chapel. Wendy anchored her fingers in her mother's palm, and they all walked to the front where the coffin lay. Her father approached the platform first, stood for a long silent moment, like a man studying a mountain trail before nightfall, committing to memory every last detail. Mark and Davey were next. Julia noted how similar their postures were, backs straight, hands folded behind them, as they paid their last respects.

Then Julia followed, with Wendy hanging back, stepping on her heels. Julia forced her attention forward, made herself look into the satin lined box. She sighed with relief; that was not her mother lying there entombed. It was a hologram, a replica, a sculpture carefully but imperfectly done. For the life, that anxious, loving light that was once Bea Green, was elsewhere. Fled. Vanished. Free. But surely not trapped, waiting to be buried in the ground.

A sense of lightness rose in Julia's chest. She turned around to speak to her father, to share her relief, and in so doing, caught sight of a seeming apparition. Standing in the doorway was a familiar figure crowned with red-gold hair that gathered the sunlight and reflected it back into the room. Her eyes met and held Ted's. Her father followed her gaze, but by now the organ had begun and the mourners were filing into the chapel in readiness for the service. Julia and her family took their seats in the first pew.

The sermon was short. The rabbi had not known Bea Green well, but his congregation was filled with women like her who had spent their lives as wives and mothers, who were respected, needed and loved. There was no one who could say a bad word about Beatrice Green, the rabbi intoned. Only Bea Green, Julia thought, only that one small unempowered self that had hungered while it fed others.

"She was," the rabbi said, evoking the Yiddish phrase, "a *balabosta*, our culture's highest praise. Not a tribute to great wealth or worldly accomplishment, but to womanhood. What greater good can be said than she put the needs of others equal to and sometimes above her own? Her greatest pleasures were running a good Jewish home, taking care of her family and being a source of comfort for her friends. Now let us turn to the Bible. In Psalm 15 we read, 'Lord, who shall abide in thy tabernacle? Who shall dwell in thy holy hill? Those that walketh uprightly and worketh righteousness.'"

After the service, Julia scanned the milling crowd for

Ted, but he was nowhere to be seen. For a moment, she wondered if she had imagined his appearance. It was so unlikely that he should be there. And yet her body still felt his presence. The family was ushered out of the chapel and into a waiting limousine. The others mourners took private cars, joining the funeral cortege. The drive to the cemetery was long and slow, the string of cars linked by headlights, making its laborious way along the busy freeway.

Finally, nearly an hour later, Julia stood with her family at the side of the grave, feeling faint from the heat and the ripe smell of wilting flowers and fresh earth. The grave was covered with a green grass carpet. They no longer lowered coffins into the ground in view of the mourners; it was deemed barbaric. She remembered her grandfather's funeral; her grandmother, all wiry strength, white hair flying, an avenging fury hurling herself upon the coffin, tearing at the lid, screaming that it open, that it release *"mein mann."*

The rabbi intoned a brief prayer, and Julia and her father were each given a small handful of earth. Her father recited the prayer and let the earth fall on the coffin lid. It was her turn. She repeated the prayer after the rabbi, the shape of the Hebrew in her mouth recalling other ceremonies: the lighting of the candles on Friday night, her mother's rosy face, a white lace cloth covering her blond curls, her slender fingers wafting the prayer through the air, blessing the house, the family, the Sabbath. Julia opened her hand, palm up, but could not release the bit of earth. Her mind willed release but her body would not obey. The resistance set up a trembling, freezing her hand, her wrist, moving up her arm and shoulder like an icy stream.

She felt Mark's presence as he moved close beside her, felt his nearness like a current of warmth, thawing her arm. "It's okay, Julia," he whispered. "It's okay." The same quiet voice that had carried her through her birth contractions, through her mother's cancer diagnosis, through her own suicide attempt. And she was finally able to release her handful of earth. It fell gently like the sound of a soft summer rain.

Mark folded her hand in his. As their palms met, she heard the gritty sound of the earth. They stood that way, connected, through the final prayer. She felt supported, comforted by the familiar solidarity and strength of family. If only it could always be this way, she thought. Simple, elemental. But what about Eros? And what about Ted? This time as she turned to leave the grave site, she was not surprised to see him as he stood decorously outside the circle of mourners. He was making his feelings clear. He was serious. Committed to their future. Was she?

As they walked by Ted, she introduced him to her father. "Dad, this is Ted Gustafson. A friend of mine." She hesitated for a hairbreadth. "From Greece."

Her father extended his hand.

"I'm sorry for your loss, sir," Ted said.

Sid Green nodded, removed a large white handkerchief, unfolded it and carefully mopped his face, all the while appraising Julia's new friend.

Mark nodded to Ted. Wendy smiled. Davey hurried on, ignoring him. "Ted was in New York," Julia explained to Mark. "He wanted to pay his respects."

Mark frowned, shifted from foot to foot uncomfortably. Emotions warred in his face. But years of practiced and necessary composure won out. This was neither the time nor the place for inquiry or confrontation. "We should go back to your dad's," he said finally. "People will be arriving soon."

"Go ahead," she said. "I'll meet you in the car in a minute." She turned to Wendy. "Go with Daddy and Grandpa."

Wendy gave her a sullen look of disapproval but let herself be led away.

When the family was out of earshot, Julia turned to Ted. "You shouldn't have come," she said.

"Are you sorry I did?" he asked.

She tried to speak, but her warring emotions silenced her. Yes, she was sorry he came. His appearance was unseemly, inappropriate. And, no, she was not sorry. What they had shared was real.

"I fell in love," he said. "So did you. Don't give up on us."

"I'm not. It's just…"

"I know," he said. "I just wanted to be here for you." His hand reached out to her, not touching. And yet she felt the caress.

"Will your father be sitting shiva?" he asked, and again she was surprised by his esoteric knowledge.

"Yes, I think so," she replied. A memory of her grandmother's house, the mirrors covered with white sheets, the wooden crates serving as chairs, the rending of clothing. As each generation moved further from the shtetl, the outward signs of mourning lessened. But Sid Green would observe the ritual in respect for Bea. Just as he would continue, Julia imagined, as throughout their life together, to do the things that mattered to her: placing a saucer under a cup, hanging up his jacket, refolding the newspaper.

As they left the grave site, the freshly watered earth pulled at Julia's shoes like quicksand. She leaned upon Ted's shoulder to free herself. A soft sound of pulling away. It took effort and will to leave this place.

As they approached the parking lot, Julia could feel the tracking gaze of her family, vivid as radar traces.

"I've got to go," she said.

"I'll be in L.A.," Ted offered.

"What?" she asked, startled.

"At the Hyatt Westwood."

"Ted I can't …"

"I know. I just want to see you." His lips brushed her cheek in farewell and he strode quickly off.

Julia hurried into the waiting limousine, meeting no one's eyes, and was gratefully absorbed into the black recesses of the car.

Ted's presence hovered over the rest of the day like a vital and uncompleted task, insistent, disturbing. Fortunately, there were many distractions. The small apartment was filled with the sound of hushed conversation, clinks of cutlery and glass, the swirl of cigarette smoke. The presence of death excited appetites; people filled paper plates with thick slices of corned beef and pastrami, mounds of potato salad and coleslaw, garlicky pickles and herring wreathed in onion. Fresh crusty rolls shed black poppy seeds on white shirts. The old men drank shot glasses of golden schnapps, and as the bottles emptied, their voices rose and the talk loosened like their belt-freed bellies. They reminisced about the Lower East Side of their boyhood, talk of pushcarts and stick ball, of shadowy girls no one would marry, jokes told in Yiddish to phlegmy laughs. The grandchildren chased each other in and out of doorways while their mothers traded stories of babysitters and part-time jobs and their fathers spoke of mortgages and baseball. By midafternoon it was a party, ending with mugs of coffee and almond studded honey cake, with handclasps and hugs as each family left, hoping they would all meet again on a happier occasion.

It took some time to set the apartment to rights. Were people careless in someone else's home, Julia wondered, or was it the stimulus of company that made their arms flail, dropping ashes and scattering food? By the time the debris of the afternoon had either been stored in the refrigerator or stuffed down the incinerator, Sid, Mark and the children settled down to watch a Yankees game on TV and Julia retreated behind the newspaper. Later, her father drove Mark and Davey back to the hotel. They would take the shuttle tomorrow morning and all would meet at the airport.

When Julia, Wendy and her father left the apartment the next morning, they were heavy with the knowledge that when Sid returned, he would be alone. How his life had changed, Julia thought, the moving center gone. Yet she knew he would seek no substitute, no replacement. He would be content to live with his memories, for he was a man who accepted life as it was given to him, enjoyed things because they were weathered and familiar. Possessions were rarely discarded; people…never.

But what about her life? Julia thought. Where was her sense of loyalty? Sacrifice? What was this self-actualizing individualism all about? Was she and her whole generation selfish, hedonistic? Or were they truth seekers? Courageous and daring?

She knew she was playing with fire. But, for her, it was a necessary fire. The world was too cold without it. And it was not simply adventure and passion she was seeking. The need lay far deeper. It was the search for truth, for wholeness. The connection between heart and head. She could no longer wear the mask of love, mime the gestures. No longer pretend. Even if this love affair with Ted would falter or end, better to have risked it. For her father the way had been clear; duty led and love followed. For her, it was like the legend of the Grail—each seeker must venture forth alone and enter the forest where it was darkest.

Her father pulled up to the airport departure ramp and all three exited. At the curb she moved into her father's arms, holding him in a close embrace. The Jungians say that deep within us resides a wise elder, a part of ourself who knows the answers to our deepest questions. When we touch that part, the answer rings through us like a crystal bell.

As Mark and Davey joined them, Wendy hugged her grandfather fiercely, her arms like a vise. In confusion and divided loyalty, she whispered, "I want to stay with you Grandpa."

"You can visit me anytime you like," Sid Green said, kissing his granddaughter's teary cheek. "Meanwhile write me lots of letters."

"I'll send you e-mails, Grandpa."

"For that I'll get a computer," he promised. Then he turned to Julia, drew her close. "Take care of yourself, darling."

As they moved apart, she met her father's eyes and saw the depths of his caring. Somehow he had intuited the situation, knew she was in trouble although this time she had not divulged it. Tears bubbled up out of her eyes and nose, unlovely, unbidden. "I'm sorry," she cried, admitting failure, asking forgiveness, this first of many shameful admissions to come.

In answer, her father cupped her face in his large hands, his fingers warm and smelling of smoke. Hours later she could still summon the feel of his fingers upon her chin.

12

The flight home was uneventful. Julia sat next to Wendy and Mark next to Davey, obviating the need for conversation. When they arrived home, Mark busied himself returning patients' phone calls while Julia unpacked. Davey immediately retreated to his room. Through the closed door, his stereo emanated the muffled beat of rap, insistent as a pacemaker. Wendy headed for her own bedroom, where she dealt out a game of solitaire, which her grandfather had just taught her. The children made themselves conspicuously absent.

Their tasks done, Julia and Mark returned to the living room. Julia sorted through the mail that had arrived in her absence; Mark read the newspaper. The only sounds were the dry shuffling of paper. The silence grew so heavy, Julia found it hard to breathe. It was like being underwater. The pressure kept building. She would have to move, surface, save herself.

She remembered a cartoon she had once seen in the *New Yorker* of two couples sitting in a living room similar to theirs, except in the center was a fully grown elephant. The caption read, "We deal with it by not talking about it." It was so apt she laughed out loud.

"What's so funny?" Mark asked.

"Nothing," she said. But she continued to laugh.

He frowned in confusion. "Are you okay?"

"No," she said. "I am not okay."

"What's wrong?"

She could see the fear in his eyes. "Everything," she said.

"Everything?" He attempted a light, placating tone. "Surely not everything."

But she would not be deflected, not this time. "Us," she said. "Things aren't right between us."

"Julia, this isn't the right time to get into that kind of a discussion. You're upset. You've just suffered a terrible loss…."

"This is the right time," she insisted. "Death makes things clearer."

"What's clear is that you're tired and hungry. We both are." He summoned his sensible take-charge medical tone. "What do you say about some dinner? Are you up to cooking or should we order some takeout?"

"I'm not hungry," she said.

"Well, I am."

"Then make something for yourself."

"I've been cooking for myself for two weeks," he said.

"Then what's one more meal?" she asked, knowing she was provoking, goading.

His voice was tight with control. "You run the house, Julia. Cooking is your responsibility, not mine."

It's your responsibility. His admonition summoned up that terrible time eight years ago. "It's your responsibility. Get up and feed her." The week after Wendy was born, deep in depression, bleeding heavily, battered from the birth, Julia had refused to get up for the baby's 2:00 a.m. feeding, had clung instead to the warmth and protection of her bed while the baby howled. "You feed her," she had begged. But Mark had given the baby her eleven o'clock feeding. It was Julia's turn. It was important, he said, that she keep normal routines, not slip into despondency and inaction.

He had cajoled and prodded, then, frustrated by her tenacity, had finally yanked her out of bed. She had lost her balance and had fallen against the edge of the dresser banging her arm and raising painful purple bruises. She had sat then, dazed, stuporous, in a rocking chair holding the baby, feeding her formula from a bottle that Mark had prepared.

Wendy had thrown up her feeding as soon as she had drained the bottle, and as Julia mopped up the sour smelling mess, Mark had knelt beside her, despairing. "Julia, what's wrong? You have a beautiful home, a healthy baby, a family. What more do you want?"

What more did she want? That was the question eight years ago. That was the question today. She stared straight ahead, as if peering into a dark chasm.

Mark paused, made wary by the weight of her silence. "Look, Julia. We're fighting over nothing. Let's go out to a restaurant."

"No. That's not it," she said seeking his gaze.

He looked away, avoiding her eyes. She crossed the room until she stood facing him, an arm's length away. Almost touching distance.

"We can't go on like this," she said quietly

"Like what?"

"Not loving each other."

He reeled back as if struck. "What do you mean? I love you. Of course I love you. I've always loved you." Then he blanched, but met her eyes. "Don't you love me?"

She stared at him. He looked so vulnerable, so shaken, as if the earth had fallen away under his feet. He had never asked that question before. It was something they took for granted, as a given. She knew how difficult it was for him to speak of it now. And her heart went out to him. She couldn't bear to hurt him. Not like this. Not now. And she was glad, suffused with relief to retrieve that long lost feeling, that tenderness. That concern. But she waited. Waited for her body to speak. Waited for the truth to rise. Waited to be certain. "I do love you," she said. "But…"

"But what?" His gaze was open, receptive. He was fully present, listening as if his life depended on it.

"But we're not in love."

"Julia, we've been married twenty years. It can't be that way."

"But it has to," she said. "It's not enough just being partners. Parents. We need the rest, too."

He sat down slowly, holding his head in his hands, shielding his face. He spoke his deepest fear, revealing the painful reality he could no longer deny. "It's that guy, isn't it? That Gustafson." He swallowed hard. "Do you love him?"

"I could."

"But do you?"

"I love what I feel with him."

"What?"

Her answer surprised her. "Freedom. Acceptance." It was as if that wise voice she had been seeking was speaking through her. Her own oracle.

"But I do accept you," he said. "I'm proud of you."

"I've had to fight you every step of the way anytime I wanted to try something new. Graduate school, the teaching job, the trip to Greece."

"And look what happened when you went," he said ruefully.

"I've always felt that you've wanted to control me. That you didn't trust me."

He was silent for a long time. "It wasn't you I didn't trust. It was me."

Now it was her turn to be bewildered. "Why?"

"Because I was nothing special. Not particularly good-looking or gifted. Just an ordinary, insecure, clumsy guy. And you were a beautiful, brilliant young woman who could charm the birds off the trees. I couldn't believe you actually wanted me. And I was sure if you got out into the world you'd meet so many more attractive men, you'd leave me."

"But I was the one who felt inadequate. I looked up to you. I thought you knew everything."

"I acted as if I did. I had to. I was treating patients my parents' age. And I did know my anatomy. At least by the book."

"You were a good doctor. You always were."

"But not a good lover," he said. His voice was low and choked, almost inaudible. She saw the effort it took him to make that admission; the pain it must have caused him each time she had turned away from him in bed. The rejection he had borne.

"It wasn't easy for you. I was so inexperienced," she said.

"So was I. You were only the second woman I'd been with. I didn't know what I was doing and I was afraid to ask. Afraid of looking like a fool. It was better to pretend that everything was all right."

Her memory flashed back to the time of Wendy's birth. This time she did not repress it, but summoned the courage to ask. "That time in the hospital when I was so depressed and you just ignored it and talked about your tennis match…"

"I didn't know what to say. How to make it better. All I could do was hope it would go away."

"And that time you pushed me and I fell?"

"Oh, God, Julia. I felt terrible. I never wanted to hurt you. I was so sorry. I am so sorry."

"Why didn't you say that?"

"I'm saying it now." He held out his hands imploringly. They reached toward hers, but he made no preemptive move, no attempt to seize her hands, to force anything. "I love you, Julia. You're the most important person in the world to me. Please don't leave me."

"Live, Julia," her mother had said. "I never did." And yet in times of need and difficulty it is the family that sustains us, supports us, helps get us through. During that long year of postpartum depression, Mark had been there for her. He had sat with her through the long silent meals, lay beside her through the teary, endless nights. He had weathered that time. Just as her father had weathered her mother's devastating illness, her bones so fragile that even an embrace could crack them.

That was family—duty, history, obligation. And it was love. An important, honorable love. How could she have forgotten that? Theirs was a love that had gone dry for lack of tending. But the roots could be watered and it might grow again.

Julia's reverie was broken by the sound of the phone ringing.

"I'll get it," Wendy called from upstairs. A minute later, she added, "It's for you."

"Take a message," Julie said.

Julia and Mark waited in silence. "It's Mr. Gustafson. He says he needs to talk to you," Wendy reported.

"Do you want to take it?" Mark asked, his voice unsteady.

"No," she said, "not now." She had made a decision and knew she must not do anything to undermine it. She moved a step closer to Mark, took one of his outstretched hands in her own.

"If all this is to mean something, we have to change. Both of us."

"I know," he said.

"We're going to need help. Are you okay with that?"

"I am." He said it as solemnly as a wedding vow. Slowly he drew her to him. They held each other cautiously, a cushion of air still separating their bodies. But she would try to bridge that distance. Honor their history. Their decency. Their family. Give their marriage sufficient time and honest effort. And a generous, forgiving heart. And after that, if joy could not be found, she would be free to leave. For then she would know that she was not running from her past but walking toward her future.

Wendy came tumbling down the stairs. "Can we eat now?"

"I think we could all use some food," Julia sighed.

"Great," Mark said. "Where do you want to go?"

"The grocery store." Julia called up the stairs. "Davey, keep an eye on Wendy. Dad and I will be right back."

Wendy, in surprising acquiescence, did not ask to join them.

As they walked to the car, Julia looked around with pleasure at the row of white stucco houses with their red tile roofs, the mowed lawns, the soft green hills in the distance. The familiar comfort of home. Wasn't it T. S. Eliot, the poet who had abandoned America for England, who had talked of going around the world, then coming back to where we started and knowing it for the first time?

Mark walked around to the passenger's side and opened the car door for her. Usually he would just flick the button. She thanked him.

"How about moussaka tonight?" she asked.

"What is it?"

"A Greek dish. Lamb and eggplant and tomato."

"Sounds good. Do you have the recipe? "

"No, I've never made it before."

"That's okay," he said. "We'll figure it out together." Then, with touching enthusiasm, he added, "It'll be fun."

As she waited for Mark to slip into the driver's seat, she glanced up at the sky. It was filled with clouds. Cumulonimbus. White topped towers with rain-gray bases. Thunder clouds. The most spectacular and dangerous of vapors. They could herald nourishing rain or searing lightning. In them the ancient Greeks, like the Hebrews before them, had listened for the voice of the gods.

Tomorrow Ted would be flying high above those clouds, searching for his lost paradise, the golden Atlantis. Sometime soon she would write to him and thank him for the wondrous days they had spent together. Tell him how much she valued that time. How much she valued him. But she now knew that she valued her marriage more.

She must try to build her own Atlantis right here on earth. In this time. In this place. A union of truth and connection. It would require dedication and sacrifice and constant vigilance. But she fervently hoped and needed to believe that it was possible.